By the Author of *The Riddle of Pen...*

Lafayette

A BUSS FROM LAFAYETTE

Dorothea Jensen

A Buss From Lafayette Teacher's Guide

Dorothea Jensen
Sienna Larson

BQB

Originally published through Create Space and Kindle Direct Publishing.

Republished in 2018 in the United States by BQB Publishing
(an imprint of Boutique of Quality Books Publishing, Inc.)
www.bqbpublishing.com

978-1-945448-13-3 (p)
978-1-945448-14-0 (e)

Library of Congress Control Number: 2017947219

Book design by Robin Krauss, www.bookformatters.com
Cover design by Ellis Dixon, www.ellisdixon.com

Praise for *A Buss From Lafayette*

"The vivid descriptions of clothing, family relationships, period-specific customs, and daily routines create a charming picture of life in 1825 . . . The characters retell stories of General Lafayette, General Washington, and others, providing readers with a thorough backdrop of history to accompany the book's main story line about Clara . . . an enjoyable introduction to the post-Revolutionary War period in America, and provides a lovely story about family, determination, and how perspective can change everything."

— The Children's Book Review

"Jensen effortlessly weaves history together with the daily trials of a girl resenting her stepmother's reminders to behave like a lady. Most school children know Lafayette's role in the Revolutionary War only superficially, and Jensen makes him come alive in a way they will remember. Historical accuracy, character development, and engaging dialogue enliven this narrative and make it an enjoyable read."

— Booklife Prize in Fiction (A Buss from Lafayette *was named one of the top ten Middle Grade entries for the Booklife Prize in Fiction.)*

"I fully believe that this is a book that most young teens, and not a few adults, will thoroughly enjoy. . .a full scale history lesson disguised as a can't put it down story."

— I Read What You Write Blog

"*A Buss from Lafayette*, by Dorothea Jensen, is a fun and fascinating read. Jensen weaves threads of historical fact within this coming-of-age story that will resonate with young audiences on many levels. Readers will love the tale of the highly relatable Clara and may even learn a thing or two about why Lafayette was so highly esteemed in America in the 1800s. This book is recommended for home and school libraries and has earned the Literary Classics Seal of Approval."

— Children's Literary Classics

Praise for *A Buss From Lafayette Teacher's Guide*

"There is no more crucial time than now to teach our children about the history of their country. The need for teachers to find ways to make history interesting is crucial. *A Buss from Lafayette* will provide not only historic background of the revolutionary time . . . but also a story that all children can identify with . . . The teachers' guide also gives many wonderful suggestions of how to integrate subjects with the historical content of this novel [and] suggests questions that challenge higher level thinking. I highly recommend this for teachers in grades 5-8."

— *Susan Elliott, Ph.D., Associate Professor,*
Quinnipiac University; Literacy and Curriculum Development.

Table of Contents

Synopsis: *A Buss From Lafayette*

Clara Hargraves, a witty, spunky, fourteen-year-old girl, has a couple of big problems: she has a new stepmother (who used to be her old maid schoolteacher aunt), and she has red hair (which means she is constantly teased). During the last week of June 1825, her small New Hampshire town is abuzz about the Revolutionary War hero Lafayette's visit to the state. What she learns about him and from him just might show Clara that her problems are not quite so terrible after all.

ISBN 978-1-939371-90-4 (paperback) $16.95
ISBN 978-1-939371-91-1 (eBook) $7.99

- Paperback or Kindle Edition from amazon.com

- Paperback or Nook Edition from barnesandnoble.com

- Kobo Edition from kobobooks.com

- iBook Edition from itunes.apple.com

- Paperback from indiebound.com

The paperback edition can also be ordered through any bookstore.

Honors/Topics

Honors: *A Buss From Lafayette*

- 2017   First Place Winner, Purple Dragonfly Book Awards, Historical Fiction Category

- 2017   Gold Medalist, Literary Classics Book Awards, Middle School/Historical Fiction Category

- 2017   Bronze Medalist, eLit Awards, Juvenile/Young Adult Category

- 2017   Recipient of the Children's Literary Classics "Seal of Approval"

- 2016   Quarter-Finalist, Booklife Prize in Fiction, Middle Grade Category (placed among the top ten MG entries)

- Listed on GratefulAmericanKids website among best history books for kids to read

Topics: *A Buss From Lafayette Teacher's Guide*

- The American Revolution

- Lafayette's role in our fight for independence

- Lafayette's 1824-5 Farewell Tour of America

- Everyday life and customs in rural America in the 1820s

Letter from the Author

Dear Teachers,

Thank you for reading *A Buss From Lafayette* with your students. I hope you will all enjoy the story and learn a lot about the American Revolution, the key role General Lafayette played in our achieving independence, and what life was like in America for young people in the early nineteenth century.

A Buss From Lafayette can be enjoyed read aloud in the classroom, read in small groups, and, of course, read individually. This curriculum guide has a variety of activities to engage young readers so that you may select those most appropriate for your students.

A Buss From Lafayette is my second work of historical fiction that teaches about the American Revolution. My first one, *The Riddle of Penncroft Farm,* was published in 1989 by Harcourt Brace Jovanovich, and has been used in classrooms across the country ever since to enrich the study of our fight for independence. The two books complement each other very well for classroom use.

On the next page, you will find details of my online platform where you and your students can learn more about these two books, their time periods and historical events, and the process of writing historical fiction. I have posted pictures, videos, audio recordings, and written information on my websites and social media to further student understanding and to bring the text and the times alive.

There are a number of audio, video, art, research, and writing activities suggested in this guide. If you would like to send me (at the e-mail address below) any works created by your students, I will post the best ones on my websites.

Finally, if you or your students have any comments, questions, or ideas for additional activities to use in the classroom when reading this book, I would love to hear from you. Also, please contact me at the e-mail address below if you would like me to video visit your classroom via Google Hangouts or FaceTime. I love to "meet" young readers!

Dorothea Jensen

jensendorothea@gmail.com

Author's Online Resources for Teachers and Students

Bublish: https://www.bublish.com/author/view/5755
Extensive background information pertaining to *A Buss from Lafayette* and some of Dorothea's other books

Websites: http://www.abussfromlafayette.com
Videos, audios, interviews, pictures of people, places, and artifacts mentioned in the story and links to all other sites
http://www.dorotheajensen.com
Information about all of Dorothea's books and links to all other sites

Book Trailer: https://youtu.be/LpUs1dAkGYs
A fun video about *A Buss From Lafayette* with great fiddle music

Pinterest: https://www.pinterest.com/dgjensen116/
Pictures of items, people, and places in Dorothea's historical fiction

Blogs: http://www.dorotheajensen.blogspot.com
Posts about writing historical fiction, among other things

Twitter: https://twitter.com/dgjensen116
Tweets about Dorothea's work, etc.

Facebook: http://www.facebook.com/dorothea.jensen.12
With separate Facebook pages for several of Dorothea's books

YouTube: Dorothea's channel
Video blogs, music, and other fun stuff (The link is too long to put here; just go to YouTube and search for *Dorothea Jensen*.)

Print Outs of Puzzles, etc: https://drive.google.com/drive/folders/1W-POCXmfgTUXyKlM-d-eHkyY2xzMVP37?usp=sharing

Color versions of all the illustrations in this guide can be found posted on the Pinterest, Facebook, websites, twitter and blog accounts given above.

About the Author

Dorothea Jensen was born in Boston, Massachusetts, and grew up in Chillicothe, Illinois (also the hometown of the creator of Zorro). She earned a B.A. in English at Carleton College and an M.A. in Education at the University of New Mexico. She has served as a Peace Corps Volunteer in South America, taught middle and high school and tutored refugees in English. She has three grown children and six grandsons.

The Riddle of Penncroft Farm, her first novel for young readers about the Revolutionary War, was published by Harcourt, Brace, Jovanovich in 1989. Named an IRA Teachers' Choices Selection soon after publication, it has been used in classrooms throughout the U.S. ever since. The winner of the Jeannette Fair Award (given by Delta Kappa Gamma, a women teachers' organization),The Loft Children's Literature Competition, and the Purple Dragonfly Book Award, Riddle was also a Master List Selection for the William Allen White Children's Book Award, the Rebecca Caudill Award, the Mark Twain Award, the South Carolina Children's Book Award, the Hoosier Young Readers Award, and the Sunshine State Young Readers Award.

In addition to writing historical fiction for kids, Dorothea also enjoys writing rhyming verse. She has created four illustrated modern Christmas stories in this genre about the high tech 21st century Izzy Elves who work for Santa. These are entitled *Tizzy, the Christmas Elf; Blizzy, the Worrywart Elf; Dizzy, the Stowaway Elf;* and *Frizzy, the S.A.D. Elf.* The first two received the Mom's Choice Award in the Level I (Ages 5-8 Years), e-book category, honoring "the best in family-friendly media." The third was "Story Monster Approved," and won the Purple Dragonfly Award Honorable Mention. The fourth won both the Red City Review Book Award and the Santa Choice Award. All are available as paperbacks, e-books, and downloadable or CD audio books through Amazon and other online stores.

An experienced actress and singer, Dorothea performed with a baroque opera company in Minneapolis, and also played many Gilbert and Sullivan contralto and mezzo roles in Philadelphia and Minneapolis. She usually lost the hero to the soprano.

Dorothea Jensen in an 1820s-style dress

Preparing to Read

- Ask if students know who General Lafayette was and what important part he played in the American Revolution. Perhaps they have heard of him through the hugely popular *Hamilton, the Musical,* in which he is called "America's Favorite Fighting Frenchman," and "the Lancelot of the Revolutionary Set." You might suggest that students keep these phrases in mind as they read *A Buss From Lafayette,* and then decide if and why they accurately describe Lafayette.

- Assess what students know about the role France played in the American Revolution.

- Share the title of the book. Define what a "buss" is (an old-fashioned English term for a playful, smacking kiss on the cheek or hand, from the French word *"un baiser,"* a kiss, pronounced *"uhn beh-zay"*). Ask the students if they can guess what the story might be about based on the title and the cover.

- Explain that the story takes place in Hopkinton, New Hampshire, in 1825. Show where it is on a map and where the locations of story events take place on the town map at the end of this guide. Discuss what it might have been like to live in a small, rural New England town in the early 1800s. Consider types of housing, population size, methods of transportation, schooling, clothing styles, occupations, and pastimes.

- Ask students if they have visited any rural towns or farms in New Hampshire or in New England, and how they compare to where they live.

- Brainstorm what students know about the American Revolution. When did it take place? What made the American colonists want to be independent? What colonies/ states were involved? What other groups (English, French, Spanish, and Native Americans) were involved? Who were some of the major figures in this war?

- What other historical fiction books have students read about the American Revolution? How did these differ from non-fiction textbooks? From whose point of view was the story written? Ask your students to think about how the author merged true events with fictional characters.

- Ask students if the state, region, or even the community they live in played a role in the Revolutionary War, either within the United States or elsewhere. If so, how and when? Do they have ancestors (American, English, French, Spanish, Native American, etc.) who might have participated in those events? Keep in mind that a number of Spanish cities in America (notably St. Augustine, Florida and Santa Fe, New Mexico) were founded more than 150 years before the Revolutionary War took place! For one surprising instance of Spanish support check out this blog post: www.dorotheajensen.blogspot.com/2016/09/surprising-spanish-support-for-american.html.

- Have students share if they have visited any reenactment sites or attended any reenactment events where they learned about colonial America, the American Revolution, or 19th century America. Which ones? What do they remember from the visit (costumes, crafts, tools, weapons, food, cooking)? What surprised them?

- In 1824-5, Lafayette toured the United States as the "Guest of the Nation." As the last general from either side of the War of Independence still alive, he was a living link to America's past. Find out which 24 states he visited. Look at the timeline and itinerary on websites such as Wikipedia to help map his tour (search "Visit of the Marquis de Lafayette to the United States"). Keep in mind that some of these maps are schematic so the route shown might not be exactly accurate. To see a detailed, interactive map of Lafayette's 1824-5 visits to New England, check out the website created by French researcher Julien Icher under the auspices of the French Consul General in Boston. The address is *www.thelafayettetrail.com*.

- Alan Hoffman, President of the American Friends of Lafayette and an expert on Lafayette's Farewell Tour, has said that it was an event unique in American history, as it lasted for thirteen months and three million people (one quarter of the total population of the U.S. at the time) came to see him. Can your students think of any other events that might compare to this?

- Young people's lives in 1825 were both similar to and quite different from the lives of your students today. Ask them to watch for examples of these similarities and differences, such as manners, gender roles, clothing, family relationships, shopping, and schooling.

- Explain that this story takes place in 1825, so there will probably be new terms referring to clothing, food, customs, and more. Point out to the students that the author has included a glossary at the end of the book making it easy for readers to look up and understand the meanings of the old-fashioned words.

Bulletin Board Ideas

These are ideas for displays that can be prepared by you or developed in conjunction with students as a class activity or homework assignment. Choose which ideas you want to use and have the students research the information needed and create interesting displays for your classroom bulletin board. Another option is to have the students share what they already know about the topic, create a display illustrating this, and then add more information as they read *A Buss From Lafayette* and complete the relevant activities.

- What students know about the American Revolution

- Graphic organizer describing what life was like in the 1820s in New Hampshire or in your own state

- Map of General Lafayette's 1824-5 Farewell tour

- Colonies/States involved in the American Revolution

- Other countries involved in the American Revolution (allies and enemies)

- Map of where General Lafayette served during the American Revolution

- Maps of major battles during the American Revolution, both on the North American continent and elsewhere

- Pictures/graphs/maps , etc., showing what it was like to have lived in a small, rural New England town in the 1800s. Consider methods of transportation, clothing styles, shopping, architecture, schooling, occupations, pastimes, and hygiene. You may print any of the pictures Dorothea has posted online such as on www.abussfromlafayette.com or www.pinterest.com/dgjensen116, or find or create other pictures to use.

- Puns/Word Plays: as the students read the story, they can add the ones they read and come up with their own.

While Reading

A Buss From Lafayette can be read aloud to the class by you and/or students can take turns doing so. (An audiobook read by the author is in the works.) Of course, it can also be read by small reading groups or by individuals.

This guide provides pre-reading activities, vocabulary and comprehension exercises and quizzes, discussion questions and activities to complete as students progress through the story, and also post-reading cross-curricular activities. You will find a wide variety of exercises and activities has been provided. Choose the activities most suitable for your students' abilities and interests. Please note that all page numbers used refer to the 2016 paperback edition of *A Buss From Lafayette*. A number of handouts, such as charts, word searches, crossword puzzles, and graphic organizers, are included with clear instructions for their use.

The story unfolds over the span of a week so this guide is divided up by each of the seven days. The plan is for students to read all of the chapters covering a particular day before completing the provided exercises and activities.

The vocabulary exercises are designed around the words presented in the chapters covering each day. They can be completed as pre- and post-reading quizzes to measure what has been learned, or simply as exercises to learn and reinforce the vocabulary. You may choose to allow students to use their books to locate the words in the story to get clues for their meanings from the context. Many of the vocabulary words can also be found in the Glossary at the back of *A Buss From Lafayette* itself. The list of vocabulary words and a brief definition is provided at the back of this guide for teacher use, as well as the answers to all written exercises.

A short reading comprehension quiz is provided for each day of the story. These quizzes will help ensure that students have read the assignment and understood the basics of the story. For more in-depth comprehension and learning, these are followed by open-ended discussion questions and activities, which can be done as classroom activities, homework assignments, or longer-term projects by individuals or student teams.

Finally, there are cross-curricular projects which include actual and virtual field trip suggestions. These are designed to expand your students' knowledge of the eras and the events of both the Revolutionary War and early 19th Century America.

Tuesday, June 21, 1825 (Chapters 1-4)

Tuesday Vocabulary

abhor p. 23

infernal p. 3

renounced p. 12

astride p. 24

itinerant p. 23

reticule p. 19

bogeyman p. 24

loathe p. 23

romping p. 1

buss p. 7

mobcap p. 2

salmagundi p. 13

citified p. 13

ninnyhammer p. 15

sapskull p. 15

ferule p. 8

pate p. 2

scant p. 1

hoyden p. 1

prissy p. 1

Tuesday Vocabulary Exercise 1

Fill in the blank with the appropriate vocabulary word.

1. School teachers _____ bullying, and do everything they can to prevent it.

2. In 1936, Edward VIII _____ his title of King of England for love.

3. During the drought, there was a _____ supply of water and town residents were told to stop watering their lawns.

4. After a brief nap, the _____ puppies were found playing in their pen, chasing their tails and climbing all over each other.

5. The city of Budapest sits _____ the Danube River, with Buda on one side and Pest on the other.

6. Her older sister was too proper and _____ to wear cutoffs. She always wore frilly dresses instead.

7. Afternoon desert heat can feel _____, but in the evening it can feel quite cool.

8. Many young musicians may _____ practicing their instruments, but they know it's the only way to get better.

9. _____ farm laborers often have a difficult life working for low wages and spending much of their time away from their families.

10. The bald man wore a baseball cap to protect his _____ from the hot sun.

11. Many small children sleep with a night-light on in their room because they're afraid the _____ might snatch them away in the night.

12. Some people from big urban areas choose to vacation in the countryside where they can abandon some of their _____ ways and enjoy a more relaxed way of life.

The Marquis de Lafayette by Alonzo Chappel

Tuesday Vocabulary Exercise 2

Find the following words in the novel and try to decipher what they mean from the context. Then write the letter of the correct definition next to its corresponding vocabulary word. Use the Glossary at the back of the book for additional help.

Word   **Definition**

1 _____ buss p. 7   A) a cane, rod, or flat piece of wood used to punish children

2 _____ ferule p. 8   B) a salad of mixed vegetables and cold cuts of meat, etc.

3 _____ hoyden p. 1   C) a playful, smacking kiss

4 _____ mobcap p. 2   D) a fool

5 _____ ninnyhammer p. 15   E) a tomboy

6 _____ reticule p. 19   F) a small wrist bag used by ladies

7 _____ salmagundi p. 13   G) a loose-fitting frilly cap women often wore indoors, or outdoors under their bonnets

8 _____ sapskull p. 15   H) a fool

Tuesday Reading Comprehension Quiz

Circle the correct answer.

1. In her head, Clara refers to her stepmother Priscilla as "Prissy." She uses this nickname as a sign of _____.

    A. affection
    B. admiration
    C. respect
    D. resentment

2. In the first journal entry, Clara says that Priscilla thinks she is a _____.

    A. tomboy
    B. hoyden
    C. ferule
    D. mobcap

3. Clara's mother died of _____.

    A. consumption
    B. cancer
    C. scarlet fever
    D. smallpox

4. Clara usually takes a bath _____.

    A. Every day
    B. Every Monday and Friday night
    C. Every other day
    D. Every Saturday night

5. General Lafayette is traveling from celebrations in _____ where nearly 100,000 people gathered to see him dedicate a monument.

    A. Boston, Massachusetts
    B. Concord, New Hampshire
    C. New York City, New York
    D. Philadelphia, Pennsylvania

6. There were _____ states in America in 1825.

    A. 18

    B. 24

    C. 35

    D. 47

7. Clara wears a linen pocket around her waist instead of carrying a _____ on her wrist that was more fashionable at the time.

    A. salmagundi

    B. mobcap

    C. pinafore

    D. reticule

8. Clara is earning money for a secret plan she has by_____.

    A. Selling eggs

    B. Cleaning houses

    C. Weeding vegetable gardens

    D. Babysitting neighbors' children

9. Priscilla's birthday gift to Clara is a _____.

    A. dark green hair ribbon

    B. doll dressed in a pink dress

    C. new straw hat

    D. long white gloves

10. Dr. Flagg is _____.

    A. the most respected doctor in town

    B. loved by the children of Hopkinton

    C. an alcoholic

    D. a sober, wealthy citizen of the town

<u>Tuesday Discussion Questions and Activities</u>

1. After reading the Tuesday chapters, use the "Clara Hargraves - Character Description" handout to list some things you know about her. Consider not only how she looks, but how she feels about herself and others, how she acts and what she says. Describe some of the concerns she has. Do these seem like reasonable concerns? Explain why you feel you can or cannot relate to her.

2. General Lafayette was visiting the United States in 1824-5, only 50 years after the Revolution began, and visited all the states in the Union at that time. How many were there? Research which ones they were and the order in which they joined. When did the state you live in become one of the United States?

3. Joss says (p. 13) that one reason Lafayette helped us was that he hated the British because they killed his father. Research how Lafayette first learned about the American Revolution, what happened when he visited England before he went to America, and why both of these show that teenager Joss has oversimplified the teenager Lafayette's feelings about England.

4. Clara turns fourteen, is told she is "almost a woman" and needs to behave "in a more ladylike manner." How is she expected to behave now? How does this compare with what adults expect of fourteen-year-old girls in the 21st century?

5. Clara detests her red hair. Do you think a metal comb would actually take the "carrots" out of her hair? What do people do now to change their appearances? Find magazine advertisements for products that people buy today to change how they look. Discuss whether these modern-day products are likely to bring about the changes the buyer wants.

6. What do we learn about Dr. Flagg in Chapter 4? How would you feel if you had to be seen by Dr. Flagg for a medical emergency? Why is he is referred to as a "bogeyman?" Investigate what some other cultures consider "bogeymen."

7. Part of the fun of reading a story is predicting what will happen. As you read this novel, use the "Predicting Outcomes" handout to describe what you think will happen, then check how accurate your predictions are when you finish the story.

8. Priscilla refers to the noon meal as "dinner" and the evening meal as "supper." Eating the main meal midday was still common in New England until the early 20th century. What might have been the reasons for this? What does your family call these meals?

Clara Hargraves - Character Description

Describe Clara at the beginning of the story, citing specific examples.

```

```

What does Clara think of the following people at the beginning of the story?
Cite specific examples.

Priscilla ··▶

```

```

Dickon ··▶

```

```

Hetty ··▶

```

```

Describe some of Clara's concerns and discuss whether you think them reasonable.

```

```

Explain why you feel you can or cannot relate to her.

```

```

Predicting Outcomes

As you read *A Buss From Lafayette*, fill out the chart below by predicting what you think will happen in the story. When you finish reading the whole novel, write down what actually happens, compare this with your own predictions, and decide whether you think the book's outcomes were believable

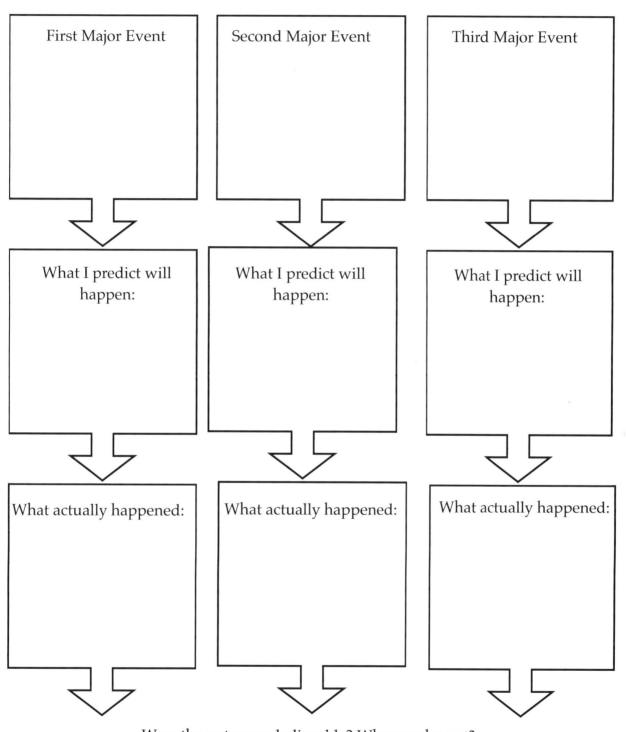

First Major Event

Second Major Event

Third Major Event

What I predict will happen:

What I predict will happen:

What I predict will happen:

What actually happened:

What actually happened:

What actually happened:

Were the outcomes believable? Why or why not?
(Write your answers on a separate sheet of paper.)

Wednesday, June 22, 1825 (Chapters 5-9)

<u>Wednesday Vocabulary</u>

addlepated p. 27   miscreant p.46   recitations p. 37

barouche p. 45   pantalettes p. 32   riled p. 58

boisterous p. 43   pinafore p. 31   savored p. 36

forestall p. 45   plaits p. 55   sedate p. 37

guffawed p. 49   predicament p. 46   wallflower p. 39

Hades p. 56   rallied p. 50   wangles p. 48

<u>Wednesday Vocabulary Exercise 1</u>

Sort the words above into parts of speech according to how they are used in the text.

Adjectives	Nouns	Verbs

Wednesday Vocabulary Exercise 2

Write sentences with the words in the "Adjectives" column. Make sure each sentence clearly demonstrates your understanding of the meaning of the vocabulary word used.

Wednesday Vocabulary Exercise 3

Provide a synonym for each vocabulary word in the "Verb" column. Explain whether or not there is a change in meaning if you were to use the synonym instead of the original word.

Verb	Synonym	Comparison of Meanings

Wednesday Vocabulary Exercise 4

Solve the crossword below using the clues provided. The answers come from this week's vocabulary list.

Across

6. something repeated aloud from memory, especially in 19th century schools

7. a person who behaves badly breaking the law (used in the story as an insult for neighboring state's residents)

8. a sleeveless apron-like garment worn over a girl's dress

9. long underpants with a frill at the bottom of each leg, worn by young girls

Down
1. a four-wheeled horse-drawn carriage with a folding cover over the rear seat only

2. the Greek underworld, associated with Christian hell

3. braids

4. a difficult, unpleasant, or embarrassing situation or problem

5. a person whom no one asks to dance and who feels excluded at a party

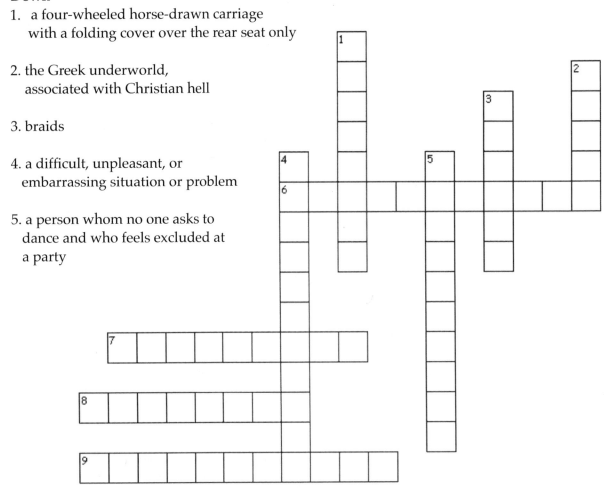

Circle whether statement is true or false.

1. Clara's family cooks all of their food in a large stone fireplace big enough for an adult to stand in.

        True   False _____

2. Clara's family has an account with Mr. Towne, a local shopkeeper, and will pay him the following week with a check.

        True   False _____

3. Clara is getting old enough that she doesn't need to wear pantalettes anymore.

        True   False _____

4. Two terms the Americans used for the British troops were "Redcoats" and "Lobsterheads."

        True   False _____

5. General Lafayette was only 18 years old when he joined the Americans in their fight for freedom.

        True   False _____

6. General Lafayette was an unfriendly, sober man.

        True   False _____

<u>Wednesday Discussion Questions and Activities</u>

1. In the story, some of the things that stand out in daily living differences between our time period and theirs include paying a bill with strawberry preserves, cooking with sugar that comes in rock-hard cone-shaped loaves, etc. Ask your students to imagine they could be teleported to 1825 New Hampshire. Use the "Time Travel" handout for them to identify some similarities and differences in daily living activities between Clara's 19th century world and their own 21st century life.

2. Two nursery rhymes are mentioned in these chapters, "Lucy Locket" and "Humpty Dumpty." Ask the students if they know the words to them, and if not, have them look them up. You will find these melodies posted at www.abussfromlafayette.com.

3. How does Clara feel about school? How does the school in the story compare with yours? Look up where the original schools were in your town or city. When were they first built? Were they one-room schoolhouses? Are any still standing? If so, how are the buildings being used now? What were the teachers like? What kind of education was needed to become a teacher? What and how were they paid? How did they "correct" students who misbehaved? Contact your local historical society to learn more about the history of your town and its schools.

4. In Chapter 7, you read about the items that can be found at Towne's General Store. What are some of these and where did they come from? What stores are similar in your town? Would you find some of the same things in these stores that Clara found at Towne's? What would be different about the modern versions of these products (in terms of packaging, storage, labeling, displaying , etc.)?

5. Have you ever heard the term "Goody Two Shoes"? How was it used and what does it mean? Look up where the term came from. What terms are used nowadays to say the same thing? Include only acceptable phrases!

6. Clara makes a word-play out of the term "Goody Two Shoes" and applies it to her cousin Henrietta. Why does she do this? What does this tell us about Clara and Hetty's relationship?

Time Travel

In the story, some things that are part of Clara's daily living (such as curtsying and bowing and paying a bill with strawberry preserves) are quite different from our modern lives. Imagine you could be teleported to 1825. What would you find to be similar and different between Clara's era and yours? The section in the center of the diagram is for experiences that you think are common to both time periods.

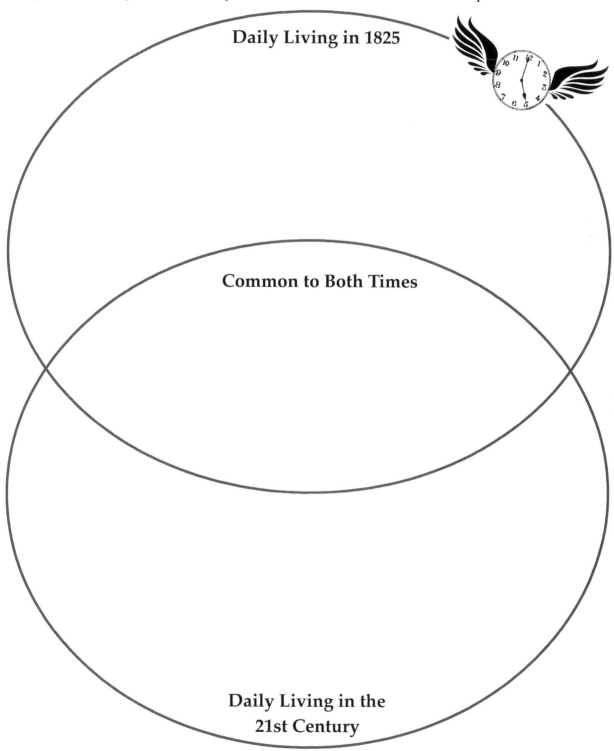

Daily Living in 1825

Common to Both Times

Daily Living in the 21st Century

Thursday, June 23, 1825 (Chapters 10-14)

<u>Thursday Vocabulary</u>

cabal p. 85	enmity p. 82	inelegance p. 73	repulsive p. 75
confinement p. 69	entourage p. 80	jaunty p. 65	seething p. 77
confounded p. 61	fripperies p. 92	nonchalant p. 73	sodden p. 72
decreed p. 62	frowsy p. 78	primping p. 79	toilette p. 78
deign p. 91	gusto p. 67	proverbial p. 63	
engrossed p. 67	impudent p. 71	repast p. 79	

<u>Thursday Vocabulary Exercise 1</u>

Look up and supply the meaning of the words below. Then on a separate piece of paper write five sentences using two of the words in each sentence. Make sure your sentences clearly demonstrate your understanding of the meaning of the vocabulary words used.

cabal	
confinement	
decreed	
entourage	
fripperies	
inelegance	
primping	
proverbial	
repast	
toilette	

Thursday Vocabulary Exercise 2

Find a synonym and an antonym for the following words.

Vocabulary Word	Synonym	Antonym
confounded		
deign		
engrossed		
enmity		
frowsy		
gusto		
impudent		
jaunty		
nonchalant		
repulsive		
seething		
sodden		

Thursday Vocabulary Exercise 3

Fill in the blanks with the most appropriate words from the Thursday Vocabulary list, modifying the words as needed to make them fit. When you finish this, look for those words in the word search below.

1. The wedding celebration included a spectacular fireworks show after a delicious
    _____.

2. As a special treat, the farmer fed the pigs leftover cake, cookies, and muffins that the animals ate with _____.

3. The famous rock star was such a diva that she traveled everywhere with a _____ of 50 people, including a chef, masseuses, hairdressers, makeup artists, a photographer, a biographer, her own personal physician, and even a florist!

4. Some of these reality shows get viewers' attention by making their participants do _____ things like eating worms and bugs.

5. Watching his favorite movie, Sam was so _____ that he didn't hear his father calling him for dinner.

6. In an attempt to contain the epidemic, the government_____ that no one could travel into or out of the area until all those infected with the virus had recovered.

7. Tom, who was very shy, tried to act _____ when he asked the girl to dance.

8. The extremely complicated math problem _____ nearly all the students, but Elizabeth managed to figure out the correct solution.

9. The _____ child was told to behave and show respect for her grandparents, or else she would be grounded for a week.

10. The haughty queen would not _____ to speak to her subjects. She insisted that a representative speak on her behalf.

11. The girls were all dressed up in their finery, but couldn't help _____ once more in front of the mirror before heading out to the party.

12. The children played so long out in the rain that their clothes were _____.

Circle the words you used above in the following word search.

```
R E P U L S I V E G H B M C
E G A R U O T N E D U P M I
N O N C H A L A N T X S Y Z
E N G R O S S E D K U B T S
D H D E C R E E D A W S C O
D Q I Y C R E P A S T U N K
O Q N P R I M P I N G I E D
S C O N F O U N D E D I G O
```

27

Respond to the following questions with a short answer.

1. Who does Clara liken to a black fly and why?

2. Who are Humpty and Dumpty in the story?

3. What are the colors of the French flag and how are they similar to or different from the American flag we have now?

4. How many children did Major Weeks have?

5. What is the special gift Hetty receives from her father that helps her to stand out when meeting General Lafayette? How does this backfire?

6. How does Clara know Dickon is wearing one of Joss's shirts?

7. What town has General Lafayette just visited, greeted by 40,000 people and the non-stop firing of two cannons on the hill in back of the State House?

8. What does Major Weeks find surprising about General Lafayette's hair and why?

9. What group of Native Americans does General Lafayette persuade to aid the Americans in their struggle against the British?

10. General Howe had boasted that the Redcoats would capture Lafayette (whom he referred to as "the boy,") and bring him as a prisoner to do what that very night?

Thursday Discussion Questions and Activities

1. Behaviors and chores are clearly divided by gender in this story. Girls are expected to behave one way and do certain chores, while boys are expected to behave differently and do other chores. What are some of the differences between the two that are mentioned in this novel? Cite specific examples. Why do you think it was this way? Is there still such a division of work between the genders where you live? What about in other parts of the world? Write an essay explaining your thoughts on differentiation of behavior and work based on your gender. Use the "Behavior and Chores" handout to organize your ideas.

2. Lafayette travels on horseback, in horse-drawn vehicles, on canal barges, and on riverboats on his tour of the twenty-four states. How is he received at each new town? Compare this to how present-day celebrities travel and how they are received by their fans.

3. New Hampshire is known as "The Granite State." In Chapter 13, we learn how the state got this nickname. What is your state's nickname and where did this come from? Pretend you are asked to write a song for your state. Write lyrics for it which include your state's nickname and some description of your state and its history.

4. In Chapter 13, Major Weeks tells the family about the Conway Cabal. What was it and what does it tell us about General Lafayette's character.

5. General Lafayette helped the Americans because he believed in liberty, but the French king at the time did not. Despite this, research why France would have been willing to support the colonists.

6. Learn more about how and where the Oneida people lived. Use "The Oneidas" handout to guide you in your research.

7. After reading about General Lee in Chapter 14, describe in your own words why he could be considered to be a traitor to the United States.

8. Clara's father mentions the French and Indian War. When did this take place? Who were the major players and what was the result for America when it ended? (See the author's blog post on the results of this war at http://dorotheajensen.blogspot.com/2016/10/french-and-indian-war.html.)

Gender-Based Behavior and Chores

Behaviors and chores are clearly divided by gender in this story. Girls are expected to behave one way and do certain chores, while boys are expected to behave differently and do other chores. What are some of the differences between the two that are mentioned in this novel? Cite specific examples. Why do you think it was this way? Is there still such a division of work between the genders where you live? What about in other parts of the world? Write an essay explaining your opinion on differentiation of behavior and work based on your gender.

Behavior & Chores for Young Women in 1820s New Hampshire	Behavior & Chores for Young Men in 1820s New Hampshire	Gender Roles Where You Live	Other Places Where Gender Roles Remain Divided

My Thoughts: _____

_____

_____

My Thesis: _____

Three Reasons for my opinion: _____

_____

_____

The Oneidas

Learn more about how and where the Oneida people lived. Conduct research to answer the first 5 questions below. Write your answers on a separate piece of paper. Then choose 3 topics from the list below to research and present to your class.

1. Learn how to pronounce "Oneida" and what the word means.

2. Where did they live and how were they organized?

3. What was their relationship to the Iroquois Confederacy?

4. Are there still Oneidas today? If so, how many, where do they live, and how are they organized?

5. What was their role in the Revolution? What effect did this have on the Iroquois Confederacy?

6. Choose three topics from the list below to research and present your findings to the class.

French Allies	French and Indian War
Longhouses	Language
Food and Drink	Storytelling
Division of Labor	Religion
Education	Toys, Games, and Sports
Weapons and Tools	Iroquois Six Nations
Arts and Crafts	Oneida Clan System
Music	Oneida Creation Story

Did you know?

The Oneidas played Lacrosse, a game invented by the Iroquois. It was a game of great skill and the field of play could be any size—even several miles long! They played it for fun, for exercise, and to settle disputes.

Friday, June 24, 1825 (Chapters 15-17)

<u>Friday Vocabulary</u>

admonish p. 105

brangle p. 106

careered p. 114

clambered p. 113

dragooned p. 105

ford p. 106

gallant p. 116

hoard p. 101

muster p. 106

nimble p. 108

oppressive p. 110

reproachfully p. 102

retorted p. 106

shucked p. 111

switched p. 99

thunderheads p. 113

ungainly p. 111

vulgar p. 108

<u>Friday Vocabulary Exercise 1</u>

Choose five words from the list above and on a separate piece of paper create tongue twisters for each one. For example, if the word starts with a "p" sound, use multiple words that start with the same "p" sound. (Example: "Peter Piper picked a peck of pickled peppers. Where's the peck of pickled peppers Peter Piper picked?") Share your tongue twister with the class, then vote with the class to select the most challenging tongue twister created. Have a competition to see which student can say that tongue twister at the fastest speed for the most times without making a mistake.

<u>Friday Vocabulary Exercise 2</u>

Find the remaining vocabulary words above in the novel. On a separate piece of paper write the sentence that each word is in. Find the best synonym to replace that word in the sentence without greatly changing the meaning of the sentence, then find the best antonym for the word. (Use a dictionary or thesaurus to help you.)

Friday Vocabulary Exercise 3

Complete the crossword by filling the blanks in the sentences below. The answers come from this week's vocabulary list.

Across

6. After blowing out a tire, the race car _____ off the course and onto the neighboring field. Needless to say, there were some very petrified cows that day!

10. The looming gray _____ confirmed that we would have to reschedule our picnic.

12. The police found a _____ of gold bars in the burglar's den.

13. Ben's father lectured him _____ for sneaking a peek at his gifts before his birthday.

14. When asked what qualified him to be the team leader, David _____ that he was the oldest and so obviously most experienced of the group.

15. We _____ the corn before putting the ears in the kettle.

16. To be successful, track and field athletes must be _____ and quick on their feet.

17. Every time they got into the car, the children would_____ over who would sit by the window.

Down

1. The cowboy _____ his horse to make it gallop faster.

2. If you cheat on a test, it's likely the principal will do more than just _____ you. You may be suspended from school.

3. There are many _____ behaviors parents need to teach their young children not to do, especially not in public!

4. The farmer led her cows across the _____ to reach the sweet grass on the other side of the creek.

5. The young boy gazed admiringly at the brave soldier and imagined himself years later as a _____ military officer.

6. When the dinner bell rang, the children _____ down from their tree house and ran inside.

7. The Boy Scouts were called to an informal _____ before the parade to make sure they were all appropriately attired.

8. People realized how _____ the dictator was when he started imprisoning all those who opposed him.

9. The children were _____ into collecting firewood for the campfire even though they wanted to go swimming.

11. Ducks and geese walk in a _____ manner compared with graceful flamingoes.

One of the many vehicles that carried Lafayette on his 1824-5 Farewell Tour, located at the Shirley-Eustis House, outside Boston, Massachusetts

Friday Reading Comprehension Quiz

Circle whether true or false, and if false, write in correct answer.

1. Clara gets the flu and is sick in bed for five days.

       True   False _____

2. Priscilla is called an "old maid" because she used to clean other people's houses.

       True   False _____

3. Joss is in charge of making charcoal for the family.

       True   False _____

4. In Chapter 15, their neighbor, Betsy, stops by to help make the strawberry preserves.

       True   False _____

5. The whisky is a small carriage, so-called because it can whisk around other vehicles.

       True   False _____

6. The French alliance with the Continentals was announced at Valley Forge.

       True   False _____

7. French Admiral D'Estaing fully cooperated with the Americans and was a great military asset at the beginning of the French Alliance.

       True   False _____

8. One of the Hargraves' horses is named Fury.

       True   False _____

9. When Clara puts her plan into action to drive the whisky all by herself, she is pleased with how smoothly the ride goes.

       True   False _____

10. Clara goes to the store to buy fabric for a new dress.

       True   False _____

<u>Friday Discussion Questions and Activities</u>

1. In Chapter 15, Clara and Priscilla talk about corporal punishment in the home and in school. Research what the laws are for your state. What do you think of them? Break up the class into two groups and hold a debate to discuss the issue. Use the "Preparing for a Debate" handout to organize your thoughts and prepare for your presentations.

2. Priscilla mentions a gentleman she had considered marrying, but who died in the War of 1812, sometimes referred to as the "second war of independence." Research where the War of 1812 was fought, what countries were involved, what they were fighting for, and what effect it had on the new country of the United States of America. Write a paragraph about what you learn.

3. Prussian Baron von Steuben is mentioned several times in this novel. Sent by Benjamin Franklin to help the Americans fight for independence, von Steuben set up the "School of the Soldier" at Valley Forge. Research whether he was really a baron, what skills and training he brought with him to America, how the "school" worked, and what impact it had on the Revolutionary War. In *The Riddle of Penncroft Farm*, Lars and Pat learn von Steuben was a bit of a phony. ". . . instead of being some big shot with the Prussian army, he was really only a captain and hadn't done any soldiering for years. And get this—it says that Ben Franklin helped fake the guy's papers so Congress would accept his help!" Why would Franklin do this?

4. As in any war, there was a lot of name-calling going on between the American troops and their supporters and British troops and their supporters. (Some examples: Whig, Tory, Revolutionist, Radical, Rebel, Loyalist, Patriot, Traitor, Redcoat, Lobsterback, Doodle.) Discuss the meaning and connotations of these terms and figure out who would call whom what.

5. In Chapter 16, we read about the alliance between the American and French being announced at Valley Forge. One might assume everything went smoothly for the Americans during the war after that promise of aid. Was that the case? Give an example. Explain the part General Lafayette played in making the French Alliance work.

Preparing for a Debate

In Chapter 15, Clara and Priscilla talk about corporal punishment in the home and in school. Research what the laws are for your state. What do you think of them? Use this handout to organize your thoughts, then break the class into two groups (pro and con) and hold a debate.

<u>Follow these steps to prepare for a debate:</u>

1. Write down your thesis. _____

2. Brainstorm ideas first on your own and then together as a group. Designate a leader to help organize the group and ensure all ideas are heard.

    My ideas & evidence: _____

    _____

    _____

    _____

    _____

3. Select your speakers and which arguments they will present.

    My role will be:_____

4. Structure the speeches:

    A. Introduction stating your argument.

    B. Preview of the main points.

    C. Prepare for rebuttals (if you are speaking after the other group has presented).

    D. Presentation of main points. (point + explanation + evidence)

    E. Recap the main points.

Saturday, June 25, 1825 (Chapters 18-26)

<u>Saturday Vocabulary</u>

affability p. 147	dumbstruck p. 123	preened p. 130
appalled p. 150	flounced p. 128	rasping p. 125
bade p. 124	ignominious p. 157	retinue p. 124
blithely p. 132	impishly p. 128	ruefully p. 163
confer p. 123	jovial p. 147	slights p. 154
distended p. 136	languidly p. 151	stratagem p. 154
droll p. 129	loping p. 166	tormentor p. 160
drudgery p. 123	petulantly p. 138	treachery p. 155

<u>Saturday Vocabulary Exercise 1</u>

Look up the definitions for this week's vocabulary words. As you read the sentences below, first underline the vocabulary words for this week as they appear in the sentences. Do these sentences make sense? If not, on a separate page, explain what's wrong with the sentences and rewrite them to make sense still using at least one of the vocabulary words used in the sentence.

1. The headstrong girl flounced languidly out of the room to meet her guests at her birthday party.

2. The general spent all day and night locked in his office developing a droll stratagem to defeat the enemy.

3. The spoiled child preened in front of the mirror and then petulantly demanded the biggest piece of cake.

4. The traitor's treachery made everyone feel jovial.

5. After his final concert, the rock star bade farewell to his retinue.

Saturday Vocabulary Exercise 2

On a separate piece of paper, write a short story of at least 100 words using three words or more from each column on the previous page. . Underline the vocabulary words in your story.

Saturday Vocabulary Exercise 3

Circle all of Saturday's vocabulary words in the following hidden message word search. Words are placed horizontally, vertically and diagonally, both forwards and backwards, and also sometimes overlap. Write all the unused letters in order (left to right, top to bottom) in the spaces below to discover a secret message.

```
F  R  G  W  A  S  H  A  S  D  I  A  P  D  I
L  E  N  N  G  T  P  T  U  G  M  F  E  E  T
O  T  I  O  N  P  R  M  N  R  P  F  T  D  R
U  I  P  A  A  A  B  O  E  L  I  A  U  N  E
N  N  O  L  T  S  M  F  D  L  S  B  L  E  A
C  U  L  A  T  I  N  N  A  O  H  I  A  T  C
E  E  G  R  N  O  D  L  B  R  L  L  N  S  H
D  E  U  I  C  A  F  A  Y  D  Y  I  T  I  E
M  C  O  R  O  T  N  E  M  R  O  T  L  D  R
K  U  L  A  N  G  U  I  D  L  Y  Y  Y  E  Y
S  B  L  I  T  H  E  L  Y  J  O  V  I  A  L
Y  L  L  U  F  E  U  R  D  E  N  E  E  R  P
Y  R  E  G  D  U  R  D  G  N  I  P  S  A  R
S  L  I  G  H  T  S  T  T  E  W  E  R  E  L
I  K  E  F  A  T  H  E  R  A  N  D  S  O  N
```

_ _ _ _ _ _ _ _ _ _ _ _   _ _ _

_ _ _ _ _ _ _ _ _ _   _ _ _ _   _ _ _ _

_ _ _ _ _ _ _   _ _ _   _ _ _ .

39

Saturday Reading Comprehension Quiz

Circle the correct answer.

1. Who comes to visit Priscilla on Saturday morning?

    A. Dickon

    B. Dr. Lerned

    C. Mr. Towne

    D. Dr. Flagg

2. Where was the big celebration that General Lafayette was arriving from in Boston?

    A. Boston Common

    B. Boston Naval Shipyard

    C. Faneuil Hall

    D. Bunker Hill

3. What will General Lafayette be doing on the Sabbath that somewhat shocks Priscilla?

    A. He will be traveling.

    B. He will be eating with strangers.

    C. He will be laboring.

    D. He will be mustering the troops.

4. Who reminds Clara of a "tottyheaded chicken"?

    A. Aunt Priscilla

    B. Aunt Penelope

    C. Hetty

    D. Mrs. Weeks

5. What kind of dance is mentioned in the novel that Priscilla would deem too shocking for Clara to dance?

    A. Virginia reel

    B. Minuet

    C. Waltz

    D. Square dance

Saturday Discussion Questions and Activities

1. Before coming to New Hampshire, General Lafayette had just left Boston where he dedicated the Bunker Hill monument. Nearly 100,000 people came to Boston to see Lafayette and this dedication. Why would this event draw so many people?

2. As we have seen, Clara is a pun-maker. In Chapter 18, the pun she makes is about Dr. Lerned's name. Make up some puns on your own using the names of famous people of today. Use only acceptable language.

3. Dr. Lerned tells the family that there are plans to set up a school for older children. Research current laws on education in your state regulating who must attend, who provides the education, and where and what students learn? How does this differ from education in the 1820s?

4. Lafayette's full name was Marie-Joseph Paul Yves Roch Gilbert du Motier, Marquis de Lafayette. Despite being born into the aristocracy, Lafayette later dropped his title and chose to be called simply "General Lafayette." How might his commitment to the American cause have affected his decision to renounce his noble title?

5. Clara knows that first cousins were legally allowed to marry at that time. What is the law in your state about this? Why might there be a law against cousins marrying?

6. Why does Lafayette refuse to kiss Hetty's hand? What does this say about his character?

7. In Chapter 21, Clara complains that she will never be able to vote or run for office. Look up when women won the right to vote, and how that came to be. Who were some of the major figures who helped make this happen? Use the "Women's Suffrage" handout to help organize your research.

8. Many versions of the Cinderella story have been told throughout the world for hundreds of years. Have you read any versions of the Cinderella story from different cultural perspectives? Check out some versions from your library and look at the similarities and differences among them. In Chapter 20, how does Clara's life resemble the story of Cinderella?

9. Research the background of Benedict Arnold. Identify reasons why he would choose to plot against America, and why he is considered one of the greatest traitors in our history. Hold a class debate with one side identifying with the American viewpoint, and the other with the British viewpoint. Discuss why it's important to know who is telling a story so that you can understand any biases in the telling.

10. In these chapters, Clara reveals her feelings about Hetty, Priscilla, and Dickon, as well as her expectation and fear of being a wallflower at the dance. Consider how her feelings are changing about each of these people and choose the one that you can identify with the most. Then imagine you are in a similar situation and write a fictional diary entry.

11. In chapter 26, Clara and Hetty take their weekly bath on Saturday afternoon, instead of the usual Saturday night, in order to get ready for the dance. In Chapter 27, they brush their teeth with brushes made of horseradish root and brush (or comb) their hair two hundred strokes to clean it. How and why did these personal hygiene activities differ from today's?

A Parisian Ball Gown

Published May 1, 1820 for La Belle Assemblée

Women's Suffrage

In Chapter 21, Clara complains that she will never be able to vote or run for office. Voting laws in the United States have changed a lot since her time. Look up how and when women won the right to vote. Use this information to choose the correct answers from the words below.

1. _____ means the right to vote in a political election.

2. At first, only white males who _____ could vote.

3. The first women's rights convention was held in Seneca Falls, _____ in 1848 led by Lucretia Mott and Elizabeth Cady _____, and with support from African-American abolitionist _____.

4. The outcome of the _____ Falls Convention was a "_____ _____," similar to the Declaration of Independence, stating that women and all people of different races should have the same rights as white men.

5. In _____, the 15th amendment was passed allowing all men to vote, regardless of their race.

6. Two separate women's suffrage groups joined together in 1894 under the leadership of _____ to form the National American Woman Suffrage Association, which continued to push for equal voting rights for women with rallies, demonstrations, picketing, and voting attempts.

7. Alice Paul and Lucy Burns organized protests in Washington in 1917. President _____ was against women voting and Alice Paul was imprisoned.

8. It wasn't until the following year that President Wilson decided to support the _____ and with the ratification (confirmation by vote) in _____, women finally got the right to vote.

9. At the time *A Buss From Lafayette* was released (2016), women had been allowed to vote in the United States for fewer than _____ years!

50	Abraham Lincoln	New York	suffrage
100	Alice Paul	owned property	Susan B. Anthony
1870	Declaration of Sentiments	Schenectady	weapons
1920	Frederick Douglass	Seneca	were married
19th Amendment	Martha Washington	Stanton	Woodrow Wilson

Sunday, June 26, 1825 (Chapters 27-29)

<u>Sunday Vocabulary</u>

capacious p. 185   perplexed p. 176

gaggle p. 181   sanctuary p. 178

guillotine p. 190   sonorous p. 176

huzzah p. 191   summons p. 191

mortification p. 179   temerity p. 182

<u>Sunday Vocabulary Exercise</u> 1

Select the letter of the most accurate definition of each word as it is used in the text.

1. _____ perplexed   A. roomy, spacious

2. _____ sonorous   B. a place of refuge or safety, a holy place

3. _____ sanctuary   C. an exclamation of approval, similar to hurrah

4. _____ mortification   D. a machine with a vertically sliding metal blade used
                             for beheading

5. _____ gaggle   E. an order to appear before someone, particularly in
                             front of a judge

6. _____ temerity
                           F. a flock of geese, or a noisy, disorderly group

7. _____ capacious
                           G. puzzled, confused

8. _____ guillotine   H. great embarrassment or shame

9. _____ huzzah   I. deep and full-sounding

10. _____ summons   J. recklessness, audacity

Fill in the blank with the most appropriate word from the current vocabulary list.

1. The weary refugees sought _____ at the United Nations camp in the neighboring country.

2. A _____ of photographers stood outside the movie set desperate to get a great shot of the celebrity.

3. Sonia was very _____ when she saw the test questions on the board until she realized she had studied the wrong chapter.

4. When going to the beach, the pale woman covered herself in a _____ kimono to protect herself from the sun.

5. As dreadful as it sounds to be sent to the _____, it was designed by an 18th century French physician to provide a more humane method of punishment.

6. With the _____ of youth, the young man was always making dangerous choices.

7. The politician felt unbearable _____ when secrets from his past were revealed by the tabloids.

8. After a child is sent to the principal's office three times, the parents receive a _____ to come speak with the principal about their child's behavior.

9. The cello has a more _____ tone than the much smaller violin.

10. The crowd cheered, "_____!" and "hurray!" as the winning team took their victory lap.

Sunday Reading Comprehension Quiz

Choose the answer which completes each sentence correctly.

1. Joss is perplexed because_____.
   A. Clara and Hetty have a friendly conversation.
   B. he doesn't understand why he can't ride in the carriage with the others.
   C. Uncle Timothy has asked him to accompany Hetty to the store to buy sugar for their Sunday meal.
   D. he can't find his Sunday shoes to wear to church.

2. The Hopkinton church bell was made by a famous silversmith named_____.
   A. James Monroe.
   B. Henry Clay.
   C. Paul Revere.
   D. John Quincy Adams.

3. At the end of the lengthy sermon, the minister urges the congregation_____.
   A. to refrain from idle chatter on their way home.
   B. to go to the Wiggins Tavern on Monday to welcome Lafayette.
   C. to contribute to a fund to support the war veterans in town.
   D. to come back to church later that day to see Lafayette.

4. Lafayette refused to mount an immediate assault on Yorktown because_____.
   A. he felt they would be outnumbered.
   B. he wanted to wait for George Washington.
   C. his troops had insufficient ammunition to defend themselves.
   D. he wouldn't fight on a Sunday due to his religious beliefs.

5. Two tunes reported to have been played when the British surrendered were_____.
   A. "Yankee Doodle" and "The World Turned Upside Down."
   B. "Yankee Doodle" and "The Star Spangled Banner."
   C. "The Swinish Multitude" and "The World Turned Upside Down."
   D. "The Star Spangled Banner" and "God Bless America."

6. After church, Clara's family stops_____.

   A. by Dr. Lerned's house because Priscilla isn't feeling well.

   B. for Sunday dinner at the Wiggins Tavern.

   C. at Towne's General Store to buy Clara her Simeon's lead comb.

   D. for Sunday dinner at the Putney Tavern.

7. During the French Revolution, General Lafayette_____.

   A. was considered a hero by most of the French people.

   B. was imprisoned for his role in his own country's Revolution.

   C. was made President of the French Republic.

   D. was sent into exile on the island of Melba.

8. Once the French promised to support the Patriots,_____.

   A. it was obvious the Americans would win their independence.

   B. the Patriots were concerned that France would want to take over the American continent for themselves.

   C. it was clear that the Italians would join forces with America as well.

   D. it was still not clear if the Americans would win the war.

First Church, Hopkinton,
New Hampshire, 1828

Sunday Discussion Questions and Activities

1. Hopkinton's First Church, where Clara attends Sunday service, not only still exists but does indeed have a Revere bell in its steeple. Research who Paul Revere was, and what it might have meant at that time to a small town like Hopkinton, New Hampshire, to have an original Revere bell. For more information on Hopkinton's Revere bell, visit <u>firstchurchhopkinton.org/about-us/first-church-history/first-churchs-1811-paul-revere-bell/</u>.

2. One of the signers of the US Constitution was Captain Nicholas Gilman from New Hampshire. If yours was a state at that time, find out who signed from your state. If it did not come into the Union until later, choose one of the original states and find out who the signer of the Constitution was for that state. Compare your answers with what your classmates find about other states. Who signs important documents on behalf of your own state now? How is this person selected?

3. The song, "The World Turned Upside Down," is mentioned on p. 183 (a recording of the music for this song can be found at <u>www.abussfromlafayette.com</u>). Look up the lyrics to this song and explain why the British might have chosen to play it. If they did.

4. Research the history and meaning behind the song "Yankee Doodle." What did the British originally intend the lyrics to express? Why did the Americans adopt it as their own signature song, and what did the lyrics mean to them?

5. "The Revolutionary War was not a dress parade, my girl. There was never any guarantee of a happy outcome," said Elder Putney on page 191. Based on what you learn in this book and from other research, make a list of the challenges and setbacks the Patriots faced during the War.

6. Research why, where, and by whom Lafayette and his family were imprisoned.

7. "Many people opposed independence from England, after all. Such dissension tore apart families and friendships," says Elder Putney on page 191. Research why some were Loyalists, others supporters of the Revolution, and others neutral. Break up into three groups and debate the various viewpoints.

8. On page 190, Father says, ". . .it is not often we meet someone who has sacrificed so much for his belief in liberty." Write about a modern individual you consider to have sacrificed for the belief in liberty and discuss how this makes you feel.

9. In Chapter 28, we learn about General Lafayette's character from the retelling of the events at the Battle of Yorktown. Use the "General Lafayette and the Siege of Yorktown" handout to describe the events and why Lafayette can be praised for what he did *not* do, versus what he *did* do.

General Lafayette and the Siege of Yorktown

You can learn a lot about people by what they do, what they say, and what others say about them. In Chapter 28, we learn about General Lafayette's character from the retelling of the events at the Battle of Yorktown. Use the framework below to describe the events and what we learn from them about General Lafayette's character.

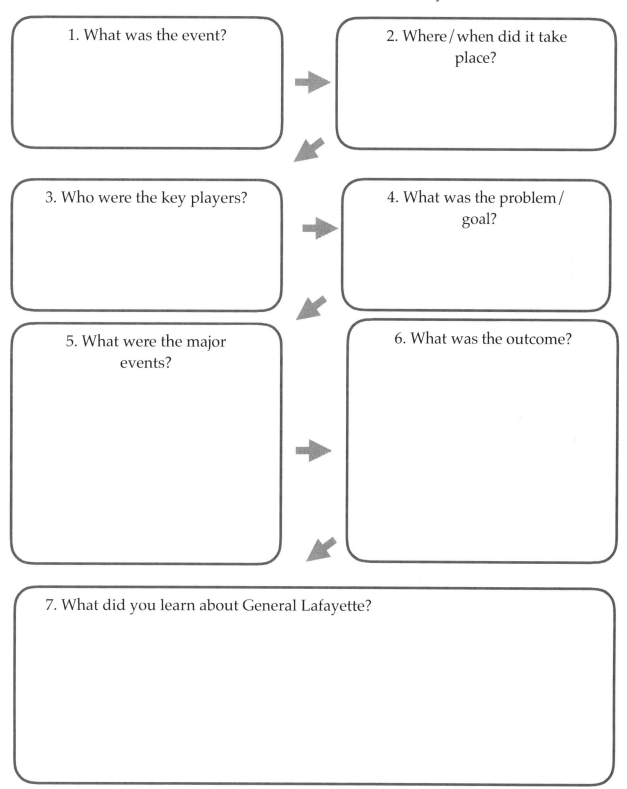

1. What was the event?

2. Where/when did it take place?

3. Who were the key players?

4. What was the problem/goal?

5. What were the major events?

6. What was the outcome?

7. What did you learn about General Lafayette?

Monday, June 27, 1825 (Chapters 30-35)

<u>Monday Vocabulary</u>

bedraggled p. 215	paltry p. 216
deliberate p. 214	precipitous p. 205
docile p. 204	recounted p. 224
gait p. 201	squall p. 228
gilt p. 214	stillborn p. 226
imperceptible p. 204	succumbed p. 216
intent p. 201	travail p. 202
intrepid p. 207	vaulting p. 222

<u>Monday Vocabulary Exercise 1</u>

Put the symbol for how well you understand each word below in the box following it.

☆ words you are sure you know

? words you think you might know

✗ words you do not know

bedraggled			paltry		
deliberate			precipitous		
docile			recounted		
gait			squall		
gilt			stillborn		
imperceptible			succumbed		
intent			travail		
intrepid			vaulting		

Monday Vocabulary Exercise 2

Find the vocabulary words in the text and guess their definitions from the context. Write down your guesses in the space provided and then look them up. Give yourself a checkmark if you're right. If not, write down the correct definition.

Vocabulary Word	Definition	✔
bedraggled		
deliberate		
docile		
gait		
gilt		
imperceptible		
intent		
intrepid		
paltry		
precipitous		
recounted		
squall		
stillborn		
succumbed		
travail		
vaulting		

Monday Vocabulary Exercise 3

Use the Monday vocabulary words to fill in the spiral crossword.

1. n. something that is intended; purpose, design   **– intent**
2. adj. done suddenly; extremely steep; abrupt, sheer
3. adj. carefully considered or studied
4. adj. easily managed or handled
5. adj. wet or dirty from being in the rain or mud
6. v. to stop trying to resist something; to yield
7. adj. not perceived by or affecting the senses
8. n. a person's manner of walking; the paces of an animal
9. v. to relate or narrate; to tell in detail
10. v. to cry out raucously
11. n. painfully difficult work; the pain of childbirth
12. adj. fearless, unafraid
13. adj. ridiculously small or worthless

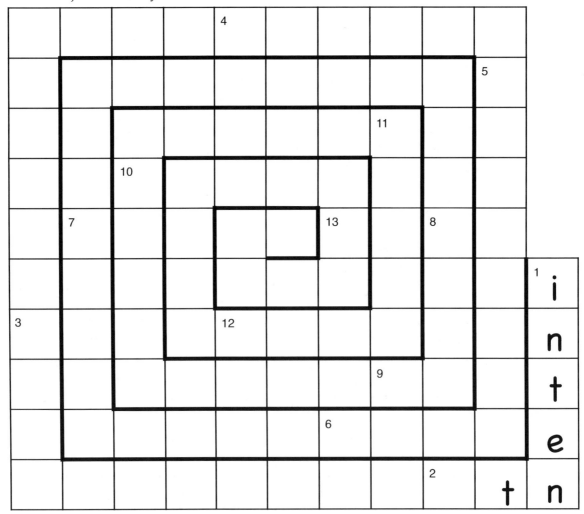

Monday Reading Comprehension Quiz Part 1

Complete the following statements with the correct information.

1. Priscilla asks Clara to read the book, _____, to her.

2. Mr. Darcy reminds Clara of_____.

3. Clara gallops into Hopkinton Village on an untrained horse to_____

_____.

4. She finds Dr. Flagg at _____.

5. General Lafayette's guilty secret is _____.

6. Dickon says Monday is a red letter day because _____

_____.

7. Dickon was looking a little stunned and overwhelmed because _____

_____.

8. Priscilla says that Clara can name her new sibling because_____

_____.

Monday Reading Comprehension Quiz Part 2

On a separate paper write who said these statements and why they are important.

1. "I think that perhaps she feels she cannot keep up with you, with the play of your mind, I mean."

2. "Women talk nonsense when they are birthing babies."

3. "She's having the baby now? You did not leave her alone, did you?"

4. "I would like to call her Rose. Caroline Rose. Would that be all right, Mother?"

1. Dr. Flagg doesn't have a very good reputation in town. We learned in Chapter 4 that he was a "semi-itinerant, often rum-soaked, Hopkinton physician who sometimes treated people in Hopkinton—mostly when none of the other doctors were available." What does he do in Chapter 31 that shows he is a better doctor than Clara thinks and perhaps makes us change our minds about him? What is surprising about this in 1820s New England?

2. Despite Clara's being in a state of high anxiety when she arrived in Contoocookville, playful words kept popping up in her head. What pun does she come up with? What do you do when you're feeling nervous or anxious?

3. While Clara is at the brook cooling off, she decides to put her lead comb to good use. Is she happy with the results? Why else is she so upset that she starts crying?

4. Clara finally does actually receive a "buss from Lafayette." How does her meeting with him affect her?

5. What does Clara learn about her stepmother in Chapter 31 that changes how she feels about her? In the final chapter, Clara calls Priscilla "Mother." Look back at the story and determine when she stopped referring to her as "Prissy" and why. Do you think moving from "Prissy" to "Mother" reveals a believable change of feeling about her stepmother by Clara?

An Old-Fashioned Doctor's Bag

Afterword

A Buss From Lafayette is a work of historical fiction. That means that the made-up part of the story is set in the distant past. This requires thorough research by the author to make sure the historic details are accurate. These details include clothing and personal grooming, food, behavior, language, political and literary references, technology, daily activities, etc. In this story, the author has built the fictional story of Clara around the actual events of General Lafayette's Farewell Tour.

In the Afterward of *A Buss From Lafayette*, Dorothea Jensen spells out what events actually happened in the story and what parts are fictional. Using the "Fact vs Fiction" handout, choose three incidents from the story and decide what details of each incident are historic fact and which are fiction. Think about how the author merged true events with fictional characters, and explain whether you think this was effective and convincing in the incidents you selected.

Additional information about historical details that the author transformed into fiction can be found at https://www.bublish.com/author/view/5755, on the author's blog, www.dorotheajensen.blogspot.com, and at www.abussfromlafayette.com.

Extension Exercise:

Choose a time period you are interested in. Research five facts and five historical details and write your own short work (2 pages) of historical fiction.

Detail of a portrait of General Lafayette on the 1824-5 Farewell Tour by Ari Scheffer

Fact versus Fiction

A Buss From Lafayette is a work of historical fiction. That means that the made-up part of the story is set in the distant past. This requires thorough research by the author to make sure the historic details are accurate. In this story, the author has built the fictional story of Clara around the actual events of General Lafayette's Farewell Tour.

In the Afterward, Dorothea Jensen spells out what events actually happened in *A Buss From Lafayette* and what parts are fictional. Choose three incidents from the story and decide what details of each incident are historic fact and which are fiction. Think about how the author merged true events with fictional characters, and explain whether or not you think this was effective and convincing in the incidents you selected.

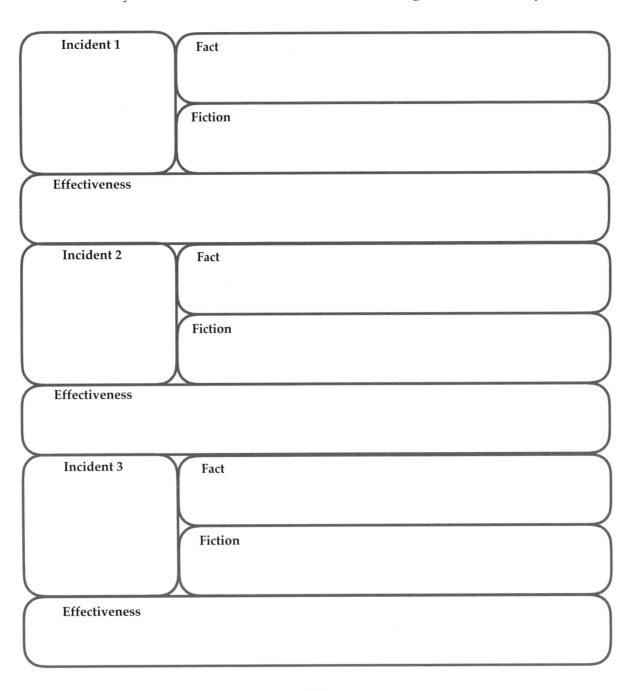

Incident 1	Fact
	Fiction

Effectiveness

Incident 2	Fact
	Fiction

Effectiveness

Incident 3	Fact
	Fiction

Effectiveness

After Reading

<u>Final Considerations</u>

1. One major theme of this story could be "coming of age" or "growing from a girl into a young woman." Thinking back on the entire story, what were the major events that most affected Clara and how did they change her? Compare the "Clara Hargraves - Character Description" handout that you completed after the Tuesday chapters to help you determine how Clara has changed over the course of the week. Use the "Clara Hargraves - Character Development" handout to identify major events that took place during the week of the story that helped Clara to learn and grow.

2. While the protagonist of the story is Clara Hargraves, it is set against the backdrop of General Lafayette's tour as the Guest of the Nation and his role in the American Revolution. Even though he only appears in one scene in this story, Lafayette is obviously one of the two main characters. In Chapter Two, Priscilla explains, "like Washington himself, Lafayette had won very few actual battles but was still a great leader," and he was indeed a great hero and leader of the Revolution in several ways. Thinking about what this means, and what you learned about Lafayette from the story, use the "General Lafayette - A Great Hero and Leader" handout, to list details under the headings *Personal Bravery in Battle, Military Leader, Mediator Between the Patriots and the French Government,* and *Petitioner for French Support.* Come up with another heading of your own to research further. Using these headings, write an essay on why or why not you believe Lafayette was a great hero and leader.

3. Dorothea Jensen has said that once she finishes a story the characters belong to the readers and they may imagine what happens next to all of them. On the "Story Extension" handout, come up with some ideas as to what this might be.

4. There are several storylines in this novel. Identify them and discuss how the author resolves them. Use the attached "Story Map" handout to illustrate one of these.

5. Pull out Tuesday's "Predicting Outcomes" sheet. See how well you predicted the story, and decide whether you believe the real outcomes were believable.

6. In *Hamilton the Musical*, Lafayette is called "America's Favorite Fighting Frenchman" and "the Lancelot of the Revolutionary Set." Discuss whether or not these phrases are accurate.

Clara Hargraves - Character Development

One major theme of this story could be "coming of age" or "growing from a girl into a young woman." Thinking back on the entire story, what were the major events that most affected Clara and how did they change her?

Write down adjectives that described Clara at the beginning of the story:

Cite major events in the story and how they changed Clara.

Event	Clara feels / changes:

Event	Clara feels / changes:

Event	Clara feels / changes:

Event	Clara feels / changes:

Describe how Clara has changed by the end of the story.

General Lafayette: A Great Leader and Hero

While Clara is the protagonist, this story is set against the backdrop of General Lafayette's Farewell Tour and his role in the American Revolution. Even though he appears in only one scene, Lafayette is obviously an important character. In Chapter Two, Priscilla explains, "like Washington himself, Lafayette had won very few actual battles but was still a great leader." Thinking about what it means to be a leader and a hero, and what you learned about Lafayette from the story, list details below under the following headings: Personal Bravery in Battle, Military Leader, Mediator between the Patriots and the French Commanders, and Petitioner for French Support. You may come up with another heading of your own as well. Using these headings, write an essay explaining why you believe he was such a great leader and hero.

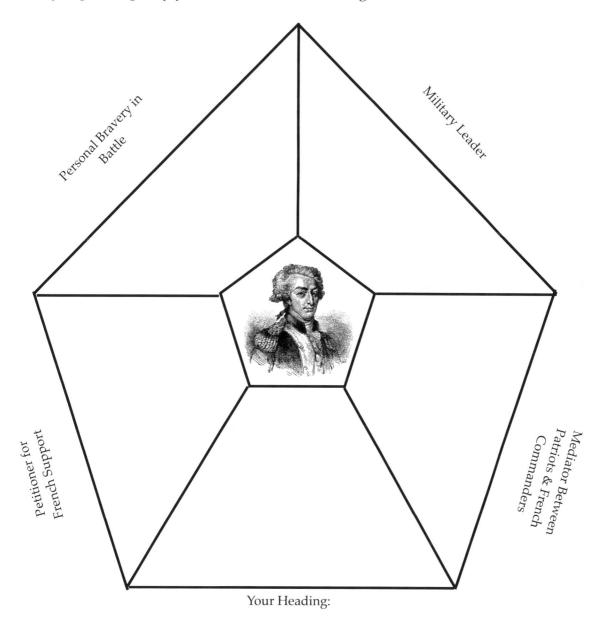

Personal Bravery in Battle

Military Leader

Petitioner for French Support

Mediator Between Patriots & French Commanders

Your Heading:

Story Extension

Dorothea Jensen has ended *A Buss From Lafayette* resolving several storylines. List as many as you can on this page, then think about how you would extend the storylines, continuing in the author's style and voice. Use another sheet of paper if needed.

Storyline 1 — Current Resolution

Storyline 2 — Current Resolution

Storyline 3 — Current Resolution

Storyline 4 — Current Resolution

Storyline 5 — Current Resolution

Brainstorm here some ideas of how you would extend the storylines. Write your extended story on a separate sheet of paper.

_____

_____

_____

_____

Story Map for
A Buss
From
Lafayette

Climax ———————————————————
          ———————————————————

Rising Action 2

_____
_____
_____
_____

Rising Action 1

_____
_____
_____

                                        Falling Action

                                        _____
                                        _____
                                        _____
                                        _____

                                        Resolution

                                        _____
                                        _____
                                        _____
                                        _____

Exposition
Characters & Traits:

_____
_____

Setting - Time & Place:

_____
_____

                                        Problem/s

                                        _____
                                        _____
                                        _____

Cross-Curricular Activities

Language Arts

• Choose one day from the story and write down all of the old-fashioned terms used, such as *gewgaw* and *riddle*. What do you think about the use of archaic words in a story like this? Do you like learning them or do you think they make the story too hard to understand? Re-write a paragraph substituting modern words for the archaic words. How does this change the story?

• Clara is a clever girl who loves to play with language by making up puns: playing with words so they have two or more meanings, or playing with similar-sounding words to humorous effect. One example on page 149 is: ". . .the name 'Procrustes' popped into my head every time I watched my mother trim the crust from a pie to fit the pie pan. Sort of a Procrustean pie, I guess." Look back through the story and see how many of Clara's puns you find. Think of others that you have heard recently in your daily conversations. Try to come up with some of your own.

• In Chapter 13, we learn that New Hampshire was first referred to as "The Granite State" in a song sung in honor of General Lafayette in Concord, New Hampshire, in 1825. Go online to www.abussfromlafayette.com to find the full text of the song and to hear the song, which is sung to an old Scottish song, "Scots Wha Ha'e Wi' Wallace Bled."

• Clara writes down her innermost thoughts in a diary. Write a diary entry for Priscilla or Henrietta, revealing how either feels about her relationship with Clara.

• *A Buss From Lafayette* is told from Clara's point of view. Pick out one scene from the story and re-write it from a different character's point of view.

• Write to the author with your questions and comments about this book. jensendorothea@gmail.com

• Write an honest review of *A Buss From Lafayette* and post it on www.amazon.com, www.goodreads.com, or other websites.

Social Studies

- Research the battles and other Revolutionary War sites in which Lafayette served. (A selection of website addresses are listed at the end of this guide.) Some of these are:

Battle of Rhode Island	Battle of Barren Hill
Battle of Brandywine	Battle of Monmouth
Winter at Valley Forge	Battle of Green Spring
Battle of Gloucester	VA Campaign & Yorktown Siege

- Discuss why foreigners, such as Frenchman Lafayette, Prussian Baron von Steuben, Bavarian-French Johann DeKalb, Poles Casimir Pulaski and Tadeusz Kosciusko, Irishman Thomas Conway, and many others came as volunteers to join the patriots in the American War for Independence. Research some of the men who came from other countries to help America. Make a chart showing their reasons for doing so, what they did to help or hinder our efforts, and what happened to them.

- Some of the foreigners who participated in the American Revolution were NOT volunteers and fought on the British side. These were soldiers "rented" from German princes by George III. Although Americans called them "Hessians," not all of them came from Hesse. Where else did they come from? Research the terms under which they ended up fighting here. Did the British pay them to do so? If not, who received the "rent" for their services and/or payment if they were injured or killed. What happened to them after the Revolution?

- Lafayette knew that his coming to America to join our War of Independence would be big news, and it was. Choose a particular event during the American Revolution where General Lafayette made an impact and research it. Write down questions you would have asked General Lafayette about the event if you were a news reporter of the time, and then answer the questions as if you were General Lafayette himself. (Make a video and send it to the author!)

- Based on what you have learned in *A Buss From Lafayette* and from other sources of information, prepare a "documentary" television interview about something he did to help us. (Battles, French Alliance, etc.)

- How did the American Revolution affect France? Write an op-ed piece about it.

- Lafayette actually was and is a more admired figure in America than he was or is in France. Conduct research into his role in the French Revolution and how that affected his popularity in that country, then and now. Write a newspaper article about what you learn from the American or from the French point of view.

• Lafayette was wed at age 16 in an arranged marriage to 14-year-old Adrienne de Noilles, whose wealthy, powerful father opposed the young Marquis going to America. *A Buss From Lafayette* focuses on Lafayette's role in the Revolution and his Farewell Tour, and his wife is only briefly mentioned. Do some research about her, her marriage to Lafayette, their children, her close call with the guillotine, her courageous stay in his prison cell, and her death. Write a news article about or do a video interview with Madame Lafayette.

Adrienne de Noailles by unknown artist

• If you live in one of the states that General Lafayette visited on his 1824-5 tour as the "Guest of the Nation," follow the itinerary he took and learn about the stops he made near where you live. Try to determine what buildings are still where he would have seen them, document them with photographs, and mark them on a map. Look at the timeline and itinerary on websites such as Wikipedia to help map his tour (search "Visit of the Marquis de Lafayette to the United States"). Keep in mind that some of these maps are schematic so the route shown might not be exactly accurate.

• If you do NOT live in one of the Farewell Tour states, research what was going on in your state (or what became your state) at that time and/or during the Revolution.

• On a map or on the internet, find the ten closest things to your school named after Lafayette. This could include memorials, statues, busts, portraits, murals, streets, buildings, schools, towns, counties, or rivers. You could start with a map posted on the website of the American Friends of Lafayette: http://www.friendsoflafayette.org/about-lafayette.html. Make a map of your own showing the location of the 10 things you have found.

Mathematics

- An estimated three million people (about one fourth of the total U.S. population at the time) came to see Lafayette when he toured America for about three hundred and eighty-eight days in 1824-5. What would be the average number of people seeing him each day? What is our current population and what would one quarter of this be? If Lafayette's Farewell Tour were today and lasted the same amount of time, how many people would have to see him each day in order to reach the same percentage of the American population that saw him on his 1824-5 tour?

- In the story, Joss buys ice skates and other items with charcoal. Clara buys her lead comb and Priscilla pays a dressmaker with strawberry jam. All this is done at Towne's store. Storekeepers in those days had to keep very complicated records. Create a page of a storekeeper's accounts showing at least ten transactions that involve three or four persons (Clara, Joss, Priscilla, a dressmaker, a tailor, etc.) Make the credit entries in black and the debits in red. Send it to jensendorothea@gmail.com for her to share online.

Health and Safety

- In the 1820s, land transportation was limited to walking, riding a horse, or riding in a horse-drawn vehicle. Look for the different forms of carriage that are mentioned in the text and look them up online (for example, barouche, whisky, chaise, gig, etc.). Discuss the pros and cons of traveling by horse and horse-drawn carriage versus modern-day transportation (speed, capacity, safety).

- Young children in the 18th and early 19th century wore pudding caps and leading strings. Look these up and learn why they were used. What would the modern-day equivalents be for these?

- Clara is worried about Priscilla or the baby dying. What was one important reason so many women died in childbirth? What was the infant mortality rate in the early 19th century in America? What is it now? What advances in health practices have been made to reduce the death rates of birthing mothers and newborn babies?

- How was canning food to preserve it different from methods used today? Do you think the method used by Priscilla kept the strawberry preserves from spoiling? How?

- Priscilla is determined that Clara learn to ride sidesaddle ("aside") instead of riding astride. Research this way of riding at that time (keeping in mind that the sidesaddles used were quite different from modern versions) and determine if this "ladylike" alternative was a safe way to ride.

Art, Music, Dance, Drama

- The town of Hopkinton, New Hampshire was founded in 1765. The houses and public buildings at the time of the novel would have been built in the Georgian, Federal, and Greek Revival styles of architecture. Conduct research to learn how architecture changed during these years and what the homes and public buildings in Clara's town might have looked like. You can see photos of some of the actual places mentioned at www.abussfromlafayette.com.

- In Chapter 12, we learn that the colors of the French flag are red, white, and blue. Have students research the flags of the three main parties involved in the American Revolution - French, British, and American. Have students draw what these flags looked like in the 1820s and identify what the colors and shapes symbolize.

- In Chapter 20 , Priscilla talks about how the fashion for dresses has changed between when Clara's parents married in 1805 or so and the time of this story in 1825. Research clothing styles for women at these times, finding and/or drawing your own pictures illustrating these changes, or draw a picture of Clara or Hetty in her ball gown.

- Changes in men's styles in clothing and hairstyles are clearly shown by what Lafayette wore as a teenager during the American Revolution and what he wears in his late sixties on his Farewell Tour of 1824-5. In chapter 22, Clara thinks that the young men at the Perkins Tavern dance look like a "flock of penguins." Research what young men wore for formal attire in 1825, finding and/or drawing your own pictures showing a young man/Dickon/Joss wearing such clothing.

- Although historians now cast doubt on the music played at the surrender of Yorktown (if any), for many years it was believed that the British band played "The World Turned Upside Down" and the American band played "Yankee Doodle." Explain the significance of both of these song titles in the context of the British surrender.

- The titles of many pieces of music are mentioned in this book, as well as names of dances. Look for the following pieces at www.abussfromlafayette.com to hear what these sounded like:"Yankee Doodle," "The World Turned Upside Down,"Go to the Devil and Shake Yourself,""Drops of Brandy,""Careless Sally,""What a Beau your Granny Was," and "Peas Upon a Trencher."

- The tune Clara dances to with Dickon is "Once Again, Sweet Richard." A video of this dance is posted on www.abussfromlafayette.com. Either try to figure out the steps to this dance and dance it with classmates, or do the Virginia Reel. (Directions and music for the Virginia Reel are on www.abussfromlafayette.com.)

- Write a script for a scene from *A Buss From Lafayette.* Act it out and make a video.

- Dorothea has posted rhyming couplets in the style of the popular musical, *Hamilton,* on www.abussfromlafayette.com. Make up a rap using these rhymes or your own and record it.

Please send any audios, videos, or artwork created for **A Buss From Lafayette** *to the author at jensendorothea@gmail.com. She will post the best ones on her websites!*

Food & Recipes

Salmagundi

Prepare a dish of salmagundi. This is a dish that originated in 17th century England and was essentially a large, decoratively laid out salad of cold cooked and raw vegetables, fruits, meats, and seafoods dressed with herbs, oil, and vinegar. Sometimes even edible flowers were added. It was usually arranged in an attractive pattern on a plate rather than tossed in a bowl. Here are some suggestions for ingredients to slice into bite-sized pieces and add to your very own salmagundi:

> *cooked shrimp, chicken, ham, beef, or turkey / hard boiled eggs / smoked or salted meats (dried beef, pepperoni etc.) / fresh tomatoes, carrots, green onions, carrots, celery, lettuce, cucumbers, lemons etc. / cooked asparagus, shallots, green beans / pickled vegetables/olives and pickles / pears, apples / almonds, walnuts, pecans*

Make sure to display the individual ingredients on the plate in a decorative way, such as circles or a geometric pattern. Season to taste and drizzle with a vinaigrette dressing.

Anadama Bread

In Chapter 13, the family enjoys anadama bread with their meal. This is an old New England bread recipe made with corn meal and molasses. There are many different versions to be found online. Here is one from an old New England cookbook:

Ingredients

1/2 cup corn meal
2 cups boiling water
2 Tablespoons shortening or butter
1/2 cup molasses

1 teaspoon salt
1 package of yeast
1/2 cup warm water
6 cups flour

Instructions

Stir the corn meal slowly into the boiling water and mix well. Add shortening or butter, molasses and salt and set aside to cool to lukewarm.

Dissolve the yeast in the warm water for about 5 minutes or until foamy.
Alternately add the yeast/water and the flour to the cooled corn meal mixture.

Knead the dough until smooth and place it in a large, covered, greased bowl in a warm place to rise. When it has doubled in size, split the dough in half, and knead it again. Shape the dough into two loaves and place in two greased bread pans. Let rise until doubled in size again.

Bake at 375^0 for 1 hour.
Slice and serve Anadama with butter. Yum!

Take a picture of the salmagundi or anadama bread that you make and send it to jensendorothea@gmail.com!

Field Trips and Further Research Suggestions

Lafayette College, in Easton, PA, has an enormous collection of paintings, documents, and artifacts related to Lafayette. Here are a couple of exhibits that can be viewed online: Marquis de Lafayette, Prisoner of Olmütz: http://sites.lafayette.edu/olmutz/
"Lafayette, We Are Here!": http://sites.lafayette.edu/lafayettewwi/

Cornell University also has Lafayette material in its collection.
http://rmc.library.cornell.edu/lafayette/exhibition/english/introduction/index.html

The American Friends of Lafayette has lots of information about Lafayette, including links to details of his Farewell Tour, on its website: http://www.friendsoflafayette.org/.

Take an online tour of an early New England house from the period. Look at the exterior and interior for details on how people built their homes, and how they lived in them. Compare what you see to how you live. If there are houses from that period in your town, visit them to see first-hand how people lived at that time.

Historic New England Houses http://www.historicnewengland.org

The Rundlet-May House in Portsmouth, NH, built in 1807, has a Rumford kitchen, used as a model for the kitchen in Clara's house. Visit it online or in person!
http://www.historicnewengland.org/historic-properties/homes/rundlet-may-house

Other houses dating back to the 1820s:

Old houses.com   http://www.oldhouses.com/historic-house-museums.htm

Traditional Home http://www.traditionalhome.com/lifestyle/travel/25-best-historic-homes-america

Old Sturbridge Village https://www.osv.org This is a particularly appropriate re-enactment site, as it portrays an era (1830) very close to that of *A Buss From Lafayette.*

Paul Revere House in Boston, MA: https://www.paulreverehouse.org

The Freedom Trail in Boston, MA: http://www.thefreedomtrail.org

American Independence Museum in Exeter, NH: https://independencemuseum.org/

Museum of the American Revolution and Colonial America at Yorktown:
http://revolutionarywarmuseum.com/Yorktown_1781.html

Museum of the American Revolution in Philadelphia, PA:
https://www.amrevmuseum.org/

Revolutionary War Battlefields: (Websites given are only a few of many online.)

Barren Hill, PA : https://en.wikipedia.org/wiki/Battle_of_Barren_Hill

Brandywine Battlefield, PA: https://en.wikipedia.org/wiki/Battle_of_Brandywine

Gloucester, NJ: https://en.wikipedia.org/wiki/Battle_of_Gloucester_(1777)

Green Spring, VA: https://worldhistoryproject.org/1781/7/6/battle-of-green-spring

Monmouth, NJ: http://www.state.nj.us/dep/parksandforests/parks/maps/monbat-brochure-map.pdf

Rhode Island: https://en.wikipedia.org/wiki/Battle_of_Rhode_Island

Valley Forge, PA: http://www.ushistory.org/ValleyForge/

Virginia Campaign andYorktown, VA: https://www.nps.gov/york/learn/historyculture/lafayette-and-the-virginia-campaign-1781.htm

In 2015, a replica was built of *L'Hermione*, the ship which brought Lafayette back to America in 1780 with news of much-needed further support from France. The reconstructed L'Hermione sailed across the Atlantic in 2015, stopping at ports on the Eastern Seaboard of the United States. http://www.hermione2015.com/#home

The L'Hermione replica arrives in
Yorktown, Virginia, in June, 2015

Historical Fiction/Non-Fiction for Kids

American Revolution

Fiction

- *Johnny Tremain* by Esther Forbes

- *The Riddle of Penncroft Farm* by Dorothea Jensen

- *The Seeds of America Trilogy* by Laurie Halse Anderson

- *Timekeepers: A Revolutionary Tale* by J. Y. Harris

Non Fiction

- *If you lived at the Time of the American Revolution* by Kay Moore

- *Traitor: the Case of Benedict Arnold* (Unforgettable Americans) by Jean Fritz

- *What is the Declaration of Independence?* by Michael C. Harris

- *Who was George Washington?* by Roberta Edwards

- *The Year of the Hangman* by Gary Blackwood

Nineteenth Century America

Fiction

- *A Gathering of Days: A New England Girl's Journal, 1830-32* by Joan W. Blos

- *Sarah Bishop* by Scott O'Dell

- *The True Confessions of Charlotte Doyle* by Avi

The bibliography at the end of A Buss From Lafayette *lists non-fiction books about both eras.*

About the Creators of This Guide

Dorothea Jensen & Sienna Larson

Dorothea Jensen is the author of *A Buss From Lafayette, The Riddle of Penncroft Farm,* and seven other books. A former English as a Second Language tutor, she also taught junior high and high school English. Dorothea earned a B.A. in English at Carleton College and an M.A. in Secondary Education from the University of New Mexico.

Sienna Larson has worked as an ESL teacher in Panama and in Ethiopia and as a homeschool teacher. She also researched and co-authored two books on international education and has created curricula for French and English language instruction for adults and children. Sienna holds a B.A. in Political Science from McGill University and an M.S. in Technology from Northern Kentucky University.

Other Books by Dorothea Jensen

Historical Fiction

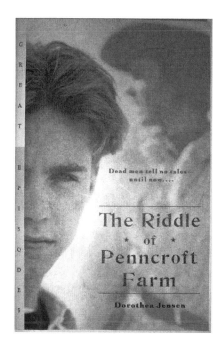

The Riddle of Penncroft Farm

Middle schooler Lars Olafson moves with his parents to the old family farm near Valley Forge, Pennsylvania. Lars is miserable until he meets Geordie, a boy whose stories of the Revolutionary War are as exciting as those of an eyewitness. Then when Lars is faced with a mystery linked to the Revolutionary War, Geordie's ghostly tales are his only chance of solving it.

". . .a fascinating merge of contemporary concerns (new school, bullies) and historical fact…A good read-aloud choice when children study the American Revolution."
—American Library Association Booklist

". . . brings the past to life while thoughtfully presenting the division between Tory and Patriot in what Jensen fairly describes as 'The First American Civil War'."
—Kirkus Children's/Young Adult

Illustrated Modern Christmas Stories in Verse

Tizzy, The Christmas Shelf Elf (Santa's Izzy Elves #1)

Naughty Owen and Alex sneak downstairs early on Christmas morning and find Tizzy, one of Santa's elves, has been packed in a present by mistake. Desperate to get back to the North Pole, Tizzy points out that Santa's sleigh is powered by the imaginations of children, and asks the two boys to use the power of their own imaginations to send him home. But how?

". . .a lovely rhyming book. . . in the tradition of the classic poem 'A Visit From St. Nicholas'. . ."*-Renee at Mother/Daughter Book Reviews*

Blizzy, the Worrywart Elf: Izzy Elves #2

Tizzy's "favorite lass," Blizzy, is the only elf who notices Tizzy is missing on Christmas morning. When she starts questioning everyone about where Tizzy could be, however, they say she is just being a worrywart. Can clever Blizzy figure out the mystery?

"What a great story, particularly for young kids . . . developing friendships and beginning to explore what it means to be a friend and care about a friend. . .lots of Izzy Elves mystery and adventure as in the first book . . ."

-A. Moore, Goodreads

Dizzy, the Stowaway Elf: Santa's Izzy Elves #3

Dizzy has heard all about his best friend Tizzy's Great Adventure and he wants to have an adventure, too! He sneaks aboard Santa's sleigh and finds even more adventure than he's dreamed of with two little boys, Stuart and Drake.

"A little elf's clandestine adventure as a stowaway on Santa's sleigh takes an unexpected turn in an engaging contemporary spin on the classic 19th-century poem, 'A Visit from St. Nicholas'. . ."

- Kirkus Reviews

Frizzy, the S.A.D. Elf: Santa's Izzy Elves #4

Frizzy styles the hair of Christmas dollies, but misses them dreadfully when Santa takes them away on Christmas Eve. (She suffers from S.A.D.: Seasonal Affection Distress.) Frizzy decides she needs to change her job so she doesn't get so attached to the toys she works on. She starts making something completely different but soon finds that her plan isn't going to work out exactly as she intended!

". . .a highly original and wonderfully developed children's book. . .

- Red City Review

Dorothea Jensen's Books in Progress

HISTORICAL FICTION

A Scalp on the Moon

In 1675, a teenaged boy who has trained his entire life for a career as an actor in Restoration London finds himself accidentally transported to Massachusetts Colony, where he knows the Puritans consider the theater to be a terrible evil. It is a time of great unrest and fear, as the Wampanoag and other Native American tribes are realizing that the English settlers are an unsettling, permanent, and growing presence in their midst. For their part, some of the superstitious colonists insist they keep seeing a scalp on the moon, a portent that something terrible is about to happen. With the outbreak of King Philip's War this portent proves all too accurate.

HISTORICAL NON FICTION

The American Revolutions: By a partial, prejudiced, and ignorant historian

Dorothea wrote this short non-fiction work long ago and is polishing it for publication. In it, she tells the story of the American Revolutions (yes, the plural is deliberate). As she says in the preface: "In a way, then, it can be said that there were *two* American Revolutions. The first was the process by which a great number of Americans "turned away" (the literal meaning of revolution, as in "revolve") from the mother country, Great Britain, and came around to the idea that America should be an independent nation. The second was the Revolutionary War, that combination of bravery, bloodshed, and blundering that made independence a reality. "

ILLUSTRATED MODERN CHRISTMAS STORY IN VERSE

Bizzy, the Know-It-All Elf, Santa's Izzy Elves #5

In this fifth installment of Santa's Izzy Elves series, the Izzy Elves and Santa Claus decide to go on vacation. Bizzy, the self-proclaimed internet whiz, finds a place for them all to visit where they can blend in nicely with the rest of the crowd. Or so he thinks!

Answers

Tuesday, June 21, 1825 (Chapters 1-4)

<u>Tuesday Vocabulary Words</u>

abhor	p. 23 v. to dislike very much
astride	p. 24 prep. with a leg in each side
bogeyman	p. 24 n. somebody considered to be especially hateful, evil, or frightening, used as a threat to frighten children into behaving well
buss	p. 7 n. or v. a playful, smacking kiss
citified	p. 13 adj. of or relating to the city, sophisticated and urban
ferule	p. 8 n. a cane, rod, or flat piece of wood used to punish children by striking them, usually on the hand.
hoyden	p. 1 n. tomboy
infernal	p. 3 adj. of or relating to hell, very unpleasant
itinerant	p. 23 adj. traveling from place to place
loathe	p. 23 v. to hate very much
mobcap	p. 2 n. a loose-fitting frilly cap women often worn indoors, or outdoors under their bonnets
ninnyhammer	p. 15 n. a fool
pate	p. 2 n. the crown of the head
prissy	p. 1 adj. having an annoying attitude of fussing too much with one's dress and behavior
renounced	p. 12 v. formally gave up something
reticule	p. 19 n. a small wrist bag used by ladies, also called a *ridicule*
romping	p. 1 adj. lively, boisterous
salmagundi	p. 13 n. a salad made of vegetables and meat dressed with oil, vinegar, and herbs
scant	p. 1 adj. barely sufficient
sapskull	p. 15 n. a fool

<u>Tuesday Vocabulary Exercise 1</u>

1. abhor or loathe 2. renounced 3. scant 4. romping 5. astride 6. prissy
8. abhor or loathe 9. itinerant   10. pate 11. bogeyman 12. citified

Tuesday Vocabulary Exercise 2

	Word		Definition
1	__C__	buss p. 7	A) a cane, rod or flat piece of wood used to punish children
2	__A__	ferule p. 8	B) a salad of mixed vegetables and cold cuts
3	__E__	hoyden p. 1	C) a playful, smacking kiss
4	__G__	mobcap p. 2	D) a fool
5	__D or H__	ninnyhammer p. 15	E) a tomboy
6	__F__	reticule p. 19	F) a small wrist bag used by ladies
7	__B__	salmagundi p. 13	G) a loose-fitting frilly cap women often wore indoors, or outdoors under their bonnets
8	__D or H__	sapskull p. 15	H) a fool

Tuesday Reading Comprehension Quiz Answers:

1. D (p. 1)
2. B (p. 1)
3. A (p. 13)
4. D (p. 24)
5. A (p. 21)
6. B (p. 12)
7. D (p. 19)
8. C (p. 19)
9. A (p. 18)
10. C (p. 23)

Wednesday, June 22, 1825 (Chapters 5-9)

<u>Wednesday Vocabulary Words</u>

addlepated	p. 27 adj. confused or stupid
barouche	p. 45 n. a four-wheeled horse-drawn carriage
boisterous	p. 43 adj. noisy and energetic
forestall	p. 45 v. to act in advance of an event to prevent it from happening
guffawed	p. 49 v. loudly and boisterously laughed
Hades	p. 56 n. the Greek and Roman underworld, associated with Christian hell
miscreant	p.46 n. a person who behaves badly breaking the law
pantalettes	p. 32 n. long underpants with a frill at the bottom of each leg, worn by girls
pinafore	p. 32 n. a sleeveless apron-like garment worn over a girl's dress
plaits	p. 55 n. braids
predicament	p. 46 n. a difficult, unpleasant or embarrassing situation or problem
rallied	p. 50 v. recovered or caused to recover in health or energy
recitations	p. 37 n. repeating something aloud from memory
riled	p. 58 v. made someone annoyed or irritated
savored	p. 36 v. tasted and completely enjoyed
sedate	p. 37 adj. calm and dignified
wallflower	p. 39 n. person who has no now rot dance with at a party
wangles	p. 48 v. obtains something by persuading or manipulating others

<u>Wednesday Vocabulary Exercise 1</u>

<u>Adjectives</u>	<u>Nouns</u>	<u>Verbs</u>
addlepated	barouche	forestall
boisterous	hades	guffawed
infernal	miscreant	plodded
sedate	pantalettes	rallied
	pinafore	riles
	plaits	savored
	predicament	wangles
	recitations	
	wallflower	

Wednesday Vocabulary Exercise 2

Sentences will vary.

Wednesday Vocabulary Exercise 3

Answers will vary. See list above for words and a brief definition of each.

Wednesday Vocabulary Exercise 4

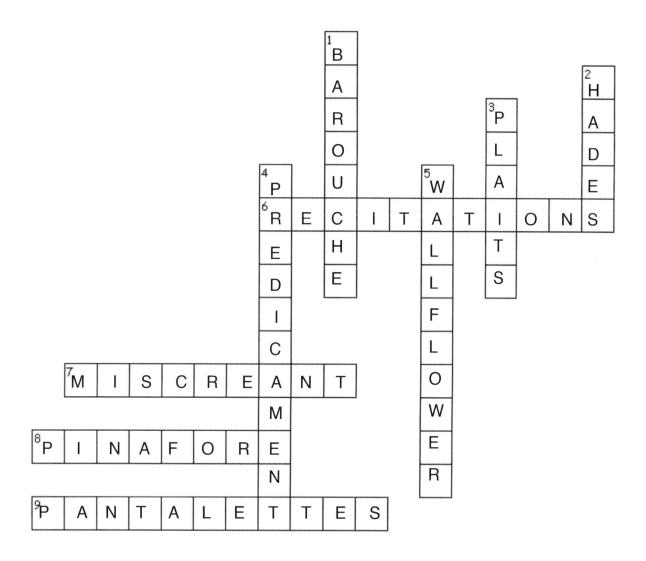

1. F - They have a Rumford range, a brick structure with two round holes for cooking, each with a closely fitted metal pot resting over a firebox below it. (p. 45)
2. F - They will pay their account with strawberry preserves. (p. 31)
3. T
4. F - They were called Redcoats and Lobsterbacks, not Lobsterheads. (p. 50)
5. F - He was 19 when he came to help the Americans. (p. 28)
6. F - He was charming and had a wonderful sense of humor. (p. 49)

Thursday, June 23, 1825 (Chapters 10-14)

cabal	p. 85 n. secret political clique
confinement	p. 69 n. childbirth
confounded	p. 61 v. confuse
decreed	p. 62 v. to order or decide in an official way
deign	p. 91 v. condescend, stoop
engrossed	p. 67 v. absorbed
enmity	p. 82 n. alienation, dislike
entourage	p. 80 n. group of people surrounding and attending to an individual
fripperies	p. 92 adj. frivolous, or nonessential clothing and accessories
frowsy	p. 78 adj. messy or shabby in personal appearance
gusto	p. 67 n. delight
impudent	p. 71 adj. brazen, cheeky
inelegance	p. 73 n. lack of elegance or dignified propriety
jaunty	p. 65 adj. buoyant, sporty
nonchalant	p. 73 adj. casual, mellow
primping	p. 79 n. trying to make yourself more attractive by making small adjustments to your hair or clothes while looking in the mirror
proverbial	p. 63 adj. commonly spoken of, widely known
repast	p. 79 n. a meal
repulsive	p. 75 adj. abhorrent, distasteful
seething	p. 77 adj. boiling, fuming
sodden	p. 72 adj. soaked
toilette	p. 78 n. process of making your personal appearance presentable

Thursday Vocabulary Words

Thursday Vocabulary Exercise 1

Students will write 5 sentences using two of the ten vocabulary words in each one.
Sentences will vary.

Thursday Vocabulary Exercise 2

Answers will vary, but this is an example of what they may look like.

Vocabulary Word	Synonym	Antonym
confound p. 61	confuse	enlighten
jaunty p. 65	buoyant, sporty	depressed
gusto p. 67	delight	indifference
engrossed p. 67	absorbed	disinterested
impudent p. 71	brazen, cheeky	humble, polite
sodden p. 72	soaked	dry
nonchalant p. 73	casual, mellow	deliberate, enthusiastic
repulsive p. 75	abhorrent, distasteful	agreeable, attractive
seething p. 77	boiling, fuming	happy, frozen
frowsy p. 78	messy, shabby	tidy
enmity p. 82	alienation, dislike	approval, friendliness
deign p. 91	condescend, stoop	rise above, be proud

Thursday Vocabulary Exercise 3

1. repast
2. gusto
3. entourage
4. repulsive
5. engrossed
6. decreed
7. nonchalant
8. confounded
9. impudent
10. deign
11. primping
12. sodden

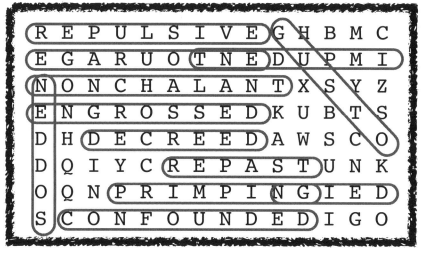

Thursday Reading Comprehension Quiz

1. Who does Clara liken to a black fly and why? *Her cousin Hetty, because she's now critical and mean toward Clara instead of being the loving cousin that she was before. p.63*

2. Who are Humpty and Dumpty? *They are the names of the Hargraves' oxen that plow the fields, etc. p. 65*

3. What are the colors of the French flag and how are they similar to or different from the colors on the American flag we have now? *They are the same colors: red, white, and blue. p. 76*

4. How many children did Major Weeks have? *Major Weeks had 13 children. p. 73*

5. What is the gift Hetty receives from her father that helps her to stand out when meeting General Lafayette? How does this backfire? *He gives her a pair of white gloves that he bought in Boston with the image of the Marquis printed on them, but Lafayette declines kissing her gloved hand because he does not want to kiss his own image. p. 76*

6. How does Clara know Dickon is wearing one of Joss' shirts? *She knows it is one of Joss' shirts because it is one she made herself and the left sleeve was not quite symmetrically attached. p. 79*

7. What town has General Lafayette just visited, greeted by 40,000 people and the non-stop firing of two cannons on the hill back of the State House? *He has just visited Concord, NH. p. 80*

8. What is surprising about General Lafayette's hair and why? *His hair is very brown and plentiful, which is quite unusual in a gentleman nearly seventy years of age. p. 83*

9. What group of Native Americans does General Lafayette persuade to aid the Americans in their struggle against the British? *General Lafayette convinces the Oneida Indians to help the Americans. p. 88*

10. General Howe had boasted that the Redcoats would capture Lafayette (whom he referred to as a "boy") and bring him as a prisoner to do what that very night? *His*

plan was to capture Lafayette and bring him to dine in Philadelphia, not something we would do with captives nowadays! p. 89

admonish	p. 105 v. warn or reprimand
brangle	p. 106 n. a loud argument
careered	p. 114 v. moved forward at a fast speed with little or no control
clambered	p. 113 v. climb up in an awkward way usually using your hands and feet
dragooned	p. 105 v. coerced someone into doing something
ford	p. 106 n. a shallow place in a river where a person may cross safely
gallant	p. 116 adj. stately, majestic, bold
hoard	p. 101 n. a stock of something someone is trying to keep secret or protected
muster	p. 106 n. a group collected in preparation for military inspection or fight
nimble	p. 108 adj. quick and light in movement or thought
oppressive	p. 110 adj. burdensome, heavy, brutal
reproachfully	p. 102 adv. doing something with expressed disapproval or disappointment
retorted	p. 106 v. responded in a sharp or rude way
shucked	p. 111 v. got rid of or removed an outer covering
switched	p. 99 v. hit or beat as with a switch or stick
thunderheads	p. 113 n. the high part of cumulus clouds that are a sign of an imminent storm
ungainly	p. 111 adj. awkward or clumsy
vulgar	p. 108 adj. unrefined, coarse, lacking in refinement

Friday, June 24, 1825 (Chapters 15-17)

Friday Vocabulary

Friday Vocabulary Exercise 1

Answers will vary. Students should have prepared five separate tongue twisters using their choice of 5 words from the provided vocabulary list. The students will share their best one with the class and compete to repeat it the fastest and the most times.

Friday Vocabulary Exercise 2

Answers will vary. With the remaining vocabulary words, students will write the sentence that the word is found in the book, and then write a synonym and an antonym.

Friday Vocabulary Exercise 3

Friday Reading Comprehension Quiz

1. False - The only flues mentioned are those of the Rumford stove. p. 97
2. False - She is called an "old maid" because she is a woman who never married. p. 100
3. True p. 100
4. False - Priscilla wears a "betsy," or ruffled collar, around her neck for modesty. p. 102
5. True p. 113
6. True p. 108
7. False - General D'Estaing and the American leaders did not work well together. p.109
8. True p. 114

9. False - The horse is afraid of the thunder and lightning and gets out of control. Dickon has to save Clara and Joss. p. 115

10. False - She goes to the store to buy the lead comb to change her red hair to black. p.

affability	p. 147 n. friendliness and easiness in approaching and speaking with
appalled	p. 150 adj. shocked or disgusted
bade	p. 124 v. past tense of to bid, to give expression to
blithely	p. 132 adv. showing lack of thought or care
confer	p. 123 v. to discuss something important before making a decision.
distended	p. 136 adj. larger and rounder than normal from internal pressure
droll	p. 129 adj. amusing or funny
drudgery	p. 123 n. boring or unpleasant work
dumbstruck	p. 123 adj. made silent by astonishment
flounced	p. 128 v. moved with exaggerated or bouncy movements
ignominious	p. 157 adj. causing shame or disgrace
impishly	p. 128 adv. playfully or mischievously
jovial	p. 147 adj. full of joy and amusement
languidly	p. 151 adv. slowly, weakly, lacking energy and force
loping	p. 166 v. an easy gait of a horse similar to a canter
petulantly	p. 138 adv. in an annoyed and angry manner when someone does not get what they want or have their way
preened	p. 130 v. devoted effort to make oneself attractive and to admire one's appearance
rasping	p. 125 adj. scratchy or harsh-sounding
retinue	p. 124 n. a group of assistants or advisers to an important person
ruefully	p. 163 adv. in a pitiable of sorrowful manner
slights	p. 154 n. acts of disrespect, such as ignoring someone or snubbing them
stratagem	p. 154 n. plans or schemes for tricking an army
tormentor	p. 160 n. one who causes annoyance, trouble or suffering
treachery	p. 155 n. betrayal of trust

117

Saturday, June 25, 1825 (Chapters 18-26)

Saturday Vocabulary

Saturday Vocabulary Exercise 1

Sentences # 1, 2 and 4 need to be rewritten by students to make sense, still using at least one of the vocabulary words in the sentence. Answers will vary.

Saturday Vocabulary Exercise 2

Stories will vary.

Saturday Vocabulary Exercise 3

Washington and Lafayette were like father and son.

Saturday Reading Comprehension Quiz Answers

1. B (p. 121)
2. D (p. 121)
3. A (p. 124)
4. B (p. 127)
5. C (p. 167)

Women's Suffrage

1. _Suffrage_ means the right to vote in a political election.

2. At first, only white males who _owned property_ could vote.

3. The first women's rights convention was held in Seneca Falls, _New York,_ in 1848 led by Lucretia Mott and Elizabeth Cady _Stanton,_ and with support from African-American abolitionist _Frederick Douglass._

4. The outcome of the _Seneca_ Falls Convention was a "_Declaration of Sentiments,_" similar to the Declaration of Independence, stating that women and all people of different races should have the same rights as white men.

5. In _1879,_ the 15th amendment was passed allowing all men to vote, regardless of their race.

6. Two separate women's suffrage groups joined together in 1894 under the leadership of _Susan B. Anthony_ to form the National American Woman Suffrage Association, which continued to push for equal voting rights for women with rallies, demonstrations, picketing, and voting attempts.

7. Alice Paul and Lucy Burns organized protests in Washington in 1917. President _Woodrow Wilson_ was against women voting and Alice Paul was imprisoned.

8. It wasn't until the following year that President Wilson decided to support the _19th Amendment_ and with the ratification (confirmation by vote) in _1920,_ women finally got the right to vote.

9. At the time _A Buss From Lafayette_ was released (2016), women had been allowed to vote in the United States for fewer than <u>100</u> years!

Sunday, June 26, 1825 (Chapters 27-29)

Sunday Vocabulary

capacious	p. 185 adj. roomy, spacious
gaggle	p. 181 n. a flock of geese, or a noisy, disorderly group
guillotine	p. 190 n. a machine with a vertically sliding metal blade used for beheading
huzzah	p. 191 interjection, an exclamation of approval, similar to hurrah
mortification	p. 179 n. great embarrassment or shame
perplexed	p. 176 adj. puzzled, confused
sanctuary	p. 178 n. a place of refuge or safety, a holy place
sonorous	p. 176 adj. deep and full-sounding
summons	. p. 191 n. an order to appear before someone, particularly in front of a judge
temerity	p. 182 n. recklessness, audacity

Sunday Vocabulary Exercise 1

1. G
2. I
3. B
4. H
5. F

6. J
7. A
8. D
9. C
10. E

Sunday Vocabulary Exercise 2

1. sanctuary
2. gaggle
3. perplexed
4. capacious
5. guillotine
6. temerity
7. mortification
8. summons
9. sonorous
10. huzzah

Sunday Reading Comprehension

1. A - p. 176
2. C - p. 176
3. B - p. 179
4. B - p. 182
5. A - p. 183 and 184
6. D - p. 186
7. B - p. 190
8. D - p. 191

Monday, June 27, 1825 (Chapters 30-35)

Monday Vocabulary

bedraggled	p. 215 adj. wet or dirty from being in the rain or mud	
deliberate	p. 214 adj. carefully considered or studied	
docile	p. 204 adj. easily managed or handled	
gait	p. 201 n. a person's manner of walking; the paces of an animal	
gilt	p. 214 adj. covered thinly with gold leaf or paint	
imperceptible	p. 204 adj. not perceived by or affecting the senses	
intent	p. 201 n. something that is intended; purpose, design	
intrepid	p. 207 adj. fearless, unafraid	
paltry	p. 216 adj. ridiculously small or worthless	
precipitous	p. 205 adj. done suddenly; extremely steep; abrupt, sheer	
recounted	p. 224 v. to relate or narrate; to tell in detail	
squall	p. 228 v. to cry out raucously	
stillborn	p. 226 adj. born dead	
succumbed	p. 216 v. to stop trying to resist something; to yield	
travail	p. 202 n. painfully difficult work; the pain and labor of childbirth	
vaulting	p. 222 v. to leap over	

Monday Vocabulary Exercise 1

Answers will vary.

Monday Vocabulary Exercise 2

Definitions will vary somewhat depending on the source used.

Monday Vocabulary Exercise 3

1. intent	8. gait
2. precipitous	9. recounted
3. deliberate	10. squall
4. docile	11. travail
5. bedraggled	12. intrepid
6. succumbed	13. paltry
7. imperceptible	

r	a	t	e	⁴d	o	c	i	l	e	
e	e	r	c	e	p	t	i	b	⁵b	
b	p	q	u	a	l	l	¹¹t	l	e	
i	m	¹⁰s	e	p	i	d	r	e	d	
l	⁷i	d	r	r	y	¹³p	a	⁸g	r	
e	d	e	t	t	l	a	v	a	a	¹i
³d	e	t	n	¹²i	l	i	a	i	g	n
s	b	n	u	o	c	e	⁹r	t	g	t
u	m	u	c	c	u	⁶s	d	e	l	e
o	t	i	p	i	c	e	r	²p	t	n

Monday Reading Comprehension Quiz Part 1

Finish the following open-ended statements with the correct information.

1. Priscilla asks Clara to read the book, _Pride and Prejudice, by Jane Austen,_ to her. p. 197

2. Whom does Mr. Darcy remind Clara of? _Dickon Weeks_ p. 197

3. Clara gallops into Hopkinton Village on an untrained horse to _fetch the doctor because her stepmother has gone into labor._ p. 201

4. She finds Dr. Flagg at _Towne's Store with a large glass of rum in his hand._ p. 203

5. General Lafayette's guilty secret is _that he is balding and wears a brown wig._ p. 216

6. Dickon says Monday is a red letter day because _Lafayette comes through town and Clara admits she was wrong._ p. 22

7. Dickon was looking a little stunned and overwhelmed because _Clara kissed him._ p. 226

8. Priscilla says that Clara can choose the name for her new sibling because _Clara was so brave and helpful in getting the doctor and her father during her stepmother's labor._ p. 228-9

Monday Reading Comprehension Quiz Part 2

Who said the following statements and why are they important?

1. "I think that perhaps she feels she cannot keep up with you, with the play of your mind, I mean."

Clara's stepmother (p. 196). Priscilla actually understands why Hetty is mean to Clara.

2. "Women talk nonsense when they are birthing babies."
Dr. Flagg (p. 206) says this to Clara for a variety of possible reasons but most likely to protect Clara from a truth she may not be aware of.

3. "She's having the baby _now_? You did not leave her _alone_, did you?"
Father (p. 210). Women delivered babies at home in those days, but attended by a midwife or doctor. Father was concerned that Priscilla had been left alone with no one to help her.

4. "I would like to call her Rose. Caroline Rose. Would that be all right, Mother?"
Clara (p. 229). Clara names the baby Rose after the rose in her hair she received from Lafayette and her red hair color, and Caroline after her deceased mother. This quote is momentous because it is the first time Clara calls her stepmother "Mother."

Map of 1825 Hopkinton, New Hampshire

Showing real and imagined locations described in *A Buss from Lafayette*

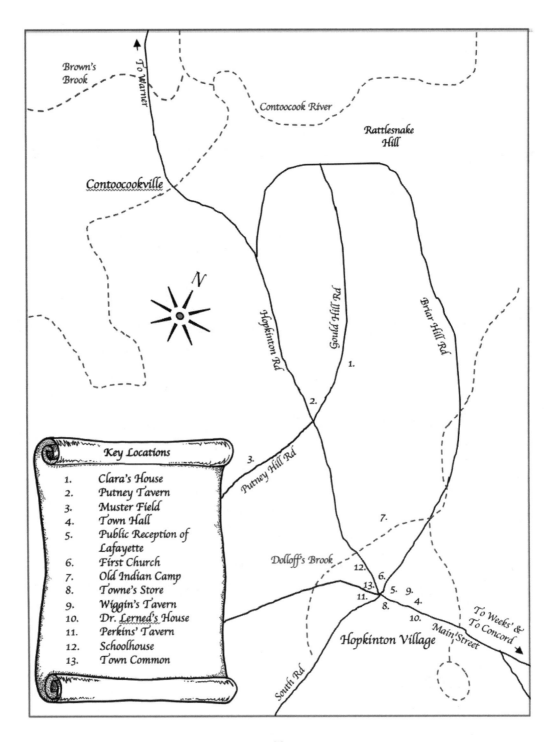

A *Real* Buss from Lafayette

*Author Dorothea Jensen receiving an actual buss from "Lafayette"
(re-enactor Mark Schneider) in Williamsburg, Virginia*